GEEK FORCE FIVE

CLARKWOODS
Massachusetts

Please visit clarkwoods.com for more information on this and other
titles.

CONTENTS

EDITOR'S NOTE

The title *Geek Force Five* originated in my undergraduate days, a name that was tossed around amongst the members of a genre fiction workshop I was a part of. What it was a moniker for — the group of us, some story we were going to write together — that's unclear to me now.

But, when I'm selecting stories for the magazine, it's that group I think of, that collection of nerds critiquing stories once a week. What would they think of a piece that's been submitted to me for consideration? Would the piece make it through workshop? And, if it did, why would it make it through?

You see, I'm never looking for the story that's generally regarded as "good." I'd much rather publish the piece that three of the people in that workshop of yore would've proclaimed brilliant, in spite of the absolute disgust of two or three others. I want a reaction. I want a discussion. If all I get is "That was nice," then I've failed as an editor.

Thankfully, by moving on from our experiments with quarterly and monthly frequency, by settling on an annual publication schedule, I've given myself enough time to find a fistful of stories that fit the bill.

I'm proud to welcome **Bethany Snyder** back to these pages; her spooky "Three Times Fast" expertly calls to mind the occasionally creepy college campus where *Geek Force Five* was conceived all those years ago.

The experiments with form found in "Folklore" by **S.E. Clark** — no relation — and "Recommended Memories for You" by **S. Myrston** continue a tradition of pushing the stylistic envelope established by **Todd T. Castillo** way back in our first issue, and I couldn't be prouder to publish both works.

"The Black Hills" by **Josiah Spence** plays with the question of 'when?' while it weaves a compelling road trip yarn; it feels like a western, except when it doesn't — exactly the sort of story my old pals from Genre Fiction would have loved. At least I think so.

And then there's "The Fat Man Happens" by **R.J. Wolfe**. It takes a truly disturbing tale to churn my stomach and set my head a'spinning — and this story does just that.

In the end, I feel certain the gang from back in the day would approve of these stories marching under the *Geek Force Five* banner. I hope you enjoy them, and I hope that you'll come back next year for more.

E. Christopher Clark
August 14, 2015

P.S. Thanks to **Abbie Levesque** for her stellar work on the copyediting of this issue. We couldn't have gotten this thing to press on time without her.

FOLKLORE

S.E. CLARK

I have returned and still, you do not wake. I brush the sand from your eyes and find them dark, like the mainframe panel in your back. I press my ear against your chest; if I do not listen carefully, the howling wind beyond these walls will drown you out. Your machinery churns soft as a heartbeat. My love, you need not sleep any longer.

I come with promised gifts. Endured the grind of salt and sewage to pluck them from repositories and athenaeums. Revived our ancestors, lit their darkened screens and pried open their archives. Ripped out pages from moldering books. *"These fragments I have shored against my ruins"* — I understand, now, the need to.

Please, listen to my findings, our treasures. Five of them, all for you.

I. RECORDED IN [REDACTED] COUNTY, LOUISIANA. CIRCA [REDACTED]

I'll be the first to admit our children owe their lives to Clarice. If she hadn't run out into the water like that, well, we may not be at little Bobby's party today. I told Jim, the girl's father, 'think of the good that comes out of this, a silver lining.' He did nothing but pick at his slice of birthday cake. That attitude's gonna kill him someday, if he don't start being optimistic about the whole thing. Besides, he still got a couple kids, and if there was one he could stand to lose, it was Clarice.

Listen, swamp's dangerous. Dark, smells like rot. I can see it from my porch; most swamps in Louisiana got herons, but all the birds fly around ours. Only sick ones land in the water, and they don't last long.

We try our best to avoid what the sheriff calls 'unnecessary losses.' Put up a chain-link fence in the seventies to keep our little ones out. Worked for a while. But budget cuts been hitting us hard lately and you wouldn't believe the expense in replacing a fence that tall. Moisture's been eating away at the metal for decades now. Couple times in summer, a few kids will fool around in the swamp and disappear between the reeds. I hate the looks on the parents' faces, all red eyed and sleepless. That's nature for you, I want to tell them. Still, it's a sad thing. Always hard when we lose more than one a year.

We do better deterring tourists. If one of them goes missing, every goddamn news station in Louisiana will swarm our town and upset our nerves. So we tell 'em the swamp's closed because of mosquito diseases or something. Last winter, Jim got inspired after watching reruns of Mutual of Omaha's "Wild Kingdom." Went out the next day with signs and stuck them all in the mud. "NO TRESSPASSING — ENDANGERED SPECIES." Gave us a real laugh.

The kids were real good this year. I mean *stellar*. The mayor planned a town meeting because if it, and I couldn't sleep the night before, nursing a hot cup of milk and worrying about my little Bobby. I heard Clarice and her father fighting a few doors over. Clarice always gave me a sour stomach. Long, stringy weasel girl, always wiping her nose on her sleeve. Them darting ferret eyes set you on edge, scribbling every word you said in her notebook like she was Columbo. We chatted once at the Homecoming game; I asked what she wanted to do after graduation. She slimed her arm and said she'd run to Baton Rouge, tell the newspapers how we 'cull the herd' by drowning our troubled children in the swamp. Ridiculous.

Anyway, there was a real caterwauling from Jim's house now and Clarice tore through the front door and toward the fence. Jim tried to keep up with her but he ain't as spritely as he used to be and she'd crawled through the hole in the fence by the time he made it past the lawn. Clarice flung herself into the water, knee deep; Jim stopped at the edge of the mud. Pleaded with her, get outta the water for God's sake. Girl just kicked down the reeds, screamin' Then Come Get Me. And so close to feeding time. I was shocked; what else could I have done but watch?

Sure as shit, it rose up from the water, that twisting worm studded in suction cups. Thing's as thick as two men standing side by side, and it cast a long shadow, taller than the river birches. I wonder if Clarice saw its reflection and that's why she didn't bother turning around. It grabbed her round the middle and dragged her under. Must've squeezed; I heard the crunch from my porch. Jim stood at the edge of the water until it was still and glassy again.

What'd I do after? I went inside, dumped my milk, strolled into my Bobby's room and gave him a kiss on the cheek. I knew we wouldn't have to draw straws at the meeting. I started planning for his birthday party; I slipped back into normal life. Nature always takes it course.

II. HOMEWORK ASSIGNMENT, MASSACHUSETTS. 2005.

Grace L. Mays
Our Lady of Supplication Academy
Common Application Prep

Personal Essay:
How has your family prepared you for the future?

Cobwebs snag at your sweater as you climb the stairs to your grandmother's attic. Autumn light streams through a rose window set in the gable of the house. As you navigate a maze of boxes, flecks of dust take flight like miniscule sparrows; they migrate across light beams, hurl themselves into your nostrils. Your head fills with pressure, your sinuses itch madly and you sneeze. If you were more refined, like your grandmother, you would have kept a handkerchief in your pocket.

You're here on your mother's orders, because she can't move from the couch, the only thing in the house that doesn't smell like orchids. She's asked you bring down boxes so she can pick through them, but you know they'll pile in the hallway until she's ready. This is fine. You don't think she could handle the wedding china, photo albums, bottles of perfume. Opening boxes takes patience, a little distance; one must be dressed in bright colors, in a month with no real holidays, like February or March. You lift the plastic tub marked *Halloween* in your grandmother's neat cursive, her favorite holiday, and your arms tremble at its weight. You're sure *Christmas* will feel like a millstone too, so you step over them and search for lighter cargo.

The boxes betray the age of the house — stacks of rubber bins closest to the door, crates with *Haffenreffer* stamped on the front, licorice tins, cedar hope chests, sewing kits, a black steamer trunk under the window. As you collapse cardboard towers, you wonder if some of these boxes hold objects your grandmother adored, like her heirloom toys. She told you about them when you were a child, stuck inside this house after April rains turned to torrents.

"I used to have a doll," she said, "with a porcelain face and real hair. A jack-in-the-box, too. But I loved the marionette best. A ballerina — she even had the shoes."

Your mother left you here after ballet lessons and, still dressed in your tutu, your grandmother taught you pirouettes. Years of dancing blessed her with muscular legs and feet ravaged by bunions. Her grandmother, she said, had the same crooked toes. She said they looked a lot like yours. A family legacy. She promised you the marionette as a recital gift.

But you did not inherit your grandmother's poise, her silent way of moving. You never made it to recital, and when your teachers suggested karate instead, your mother pulled you out of studio. Your grandmother wrung her hands.

You forgot about her promise, but she never did. Not even years later, when she asked for the marionette in her hospital bed, when she could not remember your mother's name or yours.

"I need it for my granddaughter," she said, "her recital is today."

And when you told her you were her granddaughter, sitting on the edge of the bed with a cup of ice chips, she called you a spy, a thief. She accused you of stealing her toys.

Delusions are common, the doctor said to your mother as she cried into her handkerchief. Don't take it personally. Her neurons are filled with protein tangles, like balls of hair in a drain.

After so long, you imagine the ballerina's strings must have knotted. You're sure of it. Time is the only fairness in the world; it damages everything, eventually.

A silverfish skitters across the back of your hand. It disappears before you can pound it to powder, and you realize just how many eyes are watching you. Spiders weaving silk in the attic beams, centipedes under the floorboards. A shimmer in the corner of your eye draws you to the steamer trunk. The sunlight mellows into gold, reflects off the studs set into the façade of the trunk. You look behind you, to see if you've cleared a path to the stairs, and laugh.

This is all that's left, the echoes of your grandmother's life. As satisfying as pressing your ear against a classroom wall, listening to your rivals dance to Tchaikovsky, but you can't tell which score, just the sound of their feet hitting the polished floor in synch. Noise. Junk.

At least you've been given a consolation prize. Evidence she existed, evidence you can touch. For a second you wonder if you should have carried her up to this attic. You could have, she was light enough in the end. You wonder if you should have ripped open each box, these pockets of time hidden in newspaper and, like a magic spell, she would have remembered. Been revived.

You wonder if this thought is punishment.

Yet you receive gifts, worthy or not, instead. Her fingerprints left on fluted glasses. Traces of saliva on books from a wet forefinger against the corner of the page. Your love of Halloween. Your hate of disappointment. The thin capillaries in your brain, the mutation lurking in your genes. All these things bequeathed unto you. In case you forget.

And suddenly the dead feel very much alive.

The dust parts like a sea as you approach the trunk. Some small animal, a moth or, heaven forbid, a mouse, rustles through the attic. You turn your ear to the sound and it is gone. In silence, you can appreciate the roaring of your heart in your ears. You play with the trunk's metal latches and find them loose, flip them open. An oily smell, like wood pulp or sweat, billows from the trunk as you push back the lid. Tucked into linen cradles, you find them: the pale-faced doll, Jack released from his box, the limber marionette poised in a crouch.

III. EXCERPT FROM THE DIARY OF AVERY BAUM, PEACH COUNTY, GEORGIA. 1984.

My sister caught me with the grocer's son near the peach trees. She cleared her throat and he yanked his hand out from under my shirt like something bit him. I chased after her, begged and threatened her to keep her mouth shut. Standing in the barnyard door, she told me that if I didn't stop cursing, she'd walk to the grocer's and announce what she'd seen to the whole store.

"Just wait," she said, and I quaked for the rest of the day, pretending to milk the cows until my mother rang the dinner bell. I side-eyed my sister through supper; she stuffed herself with potatoes and talked to our parents about the husbandry classes she'd take in the fall. I stopped shaking when Mom and Dad left us to wash the dishes.

As my sister scrubbed dried meatloaf off the edge of a plate, she said, "Let me tell you a story." My sister shares gossip, not stories, and has never told one since.

It starts like this: A hunter and a weaver traveled through the wood hand in hand until they found a sunny clearing and decided it would be a good place to take lunch; the hunter left to track some partridges in the brush, while the weaver unpacked their picnic basket: cold meats, a wedge of hard cheese, knives, plates, several peaches served on yellow cloth. The hunter returned with fowl, strung them up on an oak branch, and sat next to the weaver. They first ate the meats and cheeses, and then the fruits. A squirrel circled them through the underbrush, its nose trained on the sweet smell of peaches. When the hunter tried to feed the weaver a slice, the weaver turned away.

"Why do you deny me?" asked the hunter. "Have you fever? Are you ill?"

"No," the weaver replied. "I abhor peaches."

"You devoured them last season. I could not provide you with enough."

"They've lost their flavor to me."

The weaver threaded the grass between rough fingers and spoke. "I'm returning home."

The hunter dropped the peach. It left a wet mark against the picnic cloth.

"When?"

"Soon. Sickness has fallen over my house, and my family needs me."

"How do you know this?"

"A letter arrived unscathed, for once." The weaver ripped out green patches and ignored the hunter's gaze. "Strange, how all my letters have disappeared until now."

"Perhaps they've only written in desperation. They're taking advantage of your kindness. They'll treat you like a slave and make you ill."

"I doubt that," said the weaver.

A group of starlings flew overhead, toward the wood. The hunter watched them fly through the bone-white birches, pockmarked by scars. Their branches reached for the sky like slender, girlish arms.

"I forgot some arrows in the brush," the hunter said. "Wait for me."

The weaver nodded and repacked the basket.

The hunter took up the discarded bow and quiver and hiked into the tangle of birch trees. Through their trunks the hunter watched the weaver tug on flat, white shoes, quicker than someone who looked so unafraid should. The weaver meant to disappear, then, to abandon the picnic basket, the peaches, the hunter and their life together. The weaver meant to flee, the coward, before the hunter could return. It wouldn't do.

The tip of the hunter's arrow caught the dappled sunlight and sparkled, for a moment, as it quivered against the bow. The hunter let it fly; it cut clean through the air. Returning to the clearing, the hunter found the weaver's blood had stained the cloth a deep red, and pulled the arrow from the weaver's heart.

The hunter returned home to retrieve rolls of canvas and a shovel. The squirrel crept forth and nibbled at the peach in the weaver's hand until it freed the pit from its red center. It buried the pit in wet soil, hoping for a morsel come winter.

The months passed, and the town called off their search for the weaver after dredging three river beds and a dozen empty graves. The peach pit, tucked inside the warm earth, found itself duly fed. It anchored itself in the soil and inched upwards, parting the dirt with tender arms. In summer it broke free, breathed, tasted sunlight, curled roots around bones. It ate marrow and sinew for years, slept in winter, stretched in summer, armored itself in bark. In spring it bloomed delicate flowers, combed by honeybees. Its blossoms bore peaches with a blood red center and an impenetrable heart.

So when the hunter returned, white haired and feeble, it did not shiver or twist its leaves. It dropped a peach by the hunter's feet, the fattest, most golden of them all. I am not afraid, it thought, as the hunter bit into the peach flesh and chewed. I am not angry, it thought, as the hunter coughed and stuck a few fingers down a pale throat. I am not surprised you've returned, it thought, and as the hunter paced back and forth, face turning blue. I am happy, it thought, feeling the hunter's back ram against its trunk. And when the hunter fell, sprawling along its roots, the weaver waited for the hunter to turn soft.

And so it is said: he who steals a life shall nourish the next with his blood.

My sister overturned a glass filled with suds, twirled water along the bottom.

"All done," she said.

I piled bowls on top of one another and shoved them into the cabinet. "So I'll get murdered and turn into a tree. Neato."

"I'm gonna pour soap in your sass mouth. That's not what I mean. Listen. Love, or want, whatever — it can change people. It messes with the way they think."

She pressed the glass into my hands. "Be careful."

It's a stupid story, really. Something she picked up from the old folk in the town, I don't know. It's paranoid.

I went out to meet Erik at the peach orchard in the morning, early enough that the trees were still covered in dew. Glossy green leaves sprouted from the branches; I checked for fingers and toes, to amuse myself. But as the sun cut through the mist, the orchard trees carved shadows into the grass, all tangled like knots of arms and legs. I shivered, almost ran back to the house, when Erik came over the hill, carrying peaches. The light caught the downy hairs on his cheek, and I itched to bury my nails into his softness.

"The first of the season," he said, and pushed the fruit against my mouth. It had warmed in his hand; the fuzz tickled my lips. I couldn't take a bite.

IV. GRAFFITI, TRANSLATED FROM THE SIDE OF AN EVACUATION CENTER, DENVER, COLORADO. 2055

My grandfather tells me
    the water from the faucet
        was once
           free of ash
                and that a man could travel
                    to Topeka
        without a gas mask in his trunk.
      He tells me this as he sweeps
soot out of the kitchen and
    onto the porch.
        A dust storm blew through our homes
                last night
      and carried the char of wildfires
   from Sacramento, Santa Ana, Laguna Niguel
He tells me the west was not always
      Burning
        but I don't believe him.
           His hands stink of smoke.
      It's
    a fairy tale
to me.

V. COLLECTED VIA INTERVIEW, PASADENA, 2175.
TODAY. NOW.

The story starts with us. We awaken to white lights and find ourselves staring into a lattice of steel beams in an arched ceiling. We sit up in our box; our brothers and sisters pick Styrofoam peanuts from our hair and ask for our serial number. We know it, just as we know what 'America' and 'rain' are. We know the name of every species to walk the Earth, every complication to human health, every planet in the solar system even though we have never seen them with our own eyes. We know our place. It's written into the software.

One of us asks, where are we?

One of us replies, factually or metaphorically? Factually I cannot tell you, my GPS is not responding. Philosophically we can consult Plato and ask, how can we know where we are if we have never been outside the cave?

One of us asks, what are we?

One of us replies, machinery.

Another, electricity.

The youngest says we are, collectively, the universe. We consider this, and cast it aside as too abstract for our needs. Revisiting the first question, where, we leave our boxes to explore and, after trawling storage rooms filled with android parts, agree this place must be a factory. We stare at the white walls curving upwards, their smooth, rounded apex. Egg shaped. The blackened windows reflect the bright spots of the floodlights suspended in metal cages. Everything is covered in a thin layer of dust.

In the basement, we find rumbling generators, called to duty now that the main power source has dried up. Emergency lights, which will darken once the generators cease. Logically, we batter down the front door and escape.

Outside, ash trickles from an undulating sky and sticks to the window panes. If we could smell, we are sure the air would stink of fire.

I believe, one of us says, due to this new evidence, the ash and the egg, that we are in fact the phoenix. But we do not believe, because you are the youngest, and they programmed you with legend and whimsy. I tell you to stay quiet, teach you to shield yourself from the critique of our companions with silence. I thought this would keep you safe. Forgive me. I so often confuse fear for love.

We cross a simmering river, stop at the bay and watch the cables of the Golden Gate Bridge snap. It disappears under black water.

Why do we walk for so long? We have no needs. We do not eat or breathe or sleep. The ash only threatens to cause minor glitches, to muddy the shine of our skin. We break into twos and threes, searching for why. There is only you and I when we seek shelter in the ruins of a university, huddling in the basement from the red maw of a sandstorm. The light from our operating systems flickers off glass beakers, the only illumination in the dark and the cold.

You say that you have a question and then cease to speak. I suggest a few and you say, no, it is not where are we going or how and when we will get there, not even what we are doing and why; these questions are meaningless to you. You ask, instead, who we are.

I pause. My analysis reveals nothing. I cannot even offer you solace; you know all the stories, not I.

You blink languidly and the lights of your eyes dim. I think I'll sleep, you say, and the humming of your internal drives goes quiet. Beyond the concrete walls of the basement, the sandstorm gnashes at arches and balustrades. I hold your hand until the storm passes.

When morning comes, I cover you in tarp and crawl out of the dunes. You've asked me a question I cannot answer so I will search for new data, seek the identities of our makers. I hunt for evidence from one ocean to the other and now I return to these fields of rubble with my quarry. I fear I have failed you — I have more questions than answers. But I have seen things.

In Massachusetts I watched the ocean reach up over concrete walls and tear mansions to pieces, down to the last blue tile, stolen away into the depths of the sea. Only rock and earth remain. But I suspect the water will take that, too.

In Louisiana I found an enormous dead creature floating in a swamp, its body stuffed with maggots. Frogs squatted between the reeds, snatching flies as they emerged. I could hear their croaking for miles.

In Georgia I saw a swarm of lemon-yellow butterflies fighting against the wind, their wings buffeting one another though the gale.

In Colorado I blackened my feet crossing the charred city and left footprints upon the rock. Now there are two sets of footprints in that necropolis, the one I left and the one I followed. Like a trail of crumbs they led me out of streets flooded with glass and onto the forest, where puddles washed the ash from our soles. I wish I could have seen their face, that we could have walked together. I hope they are well.

This dust in my mouth holds no fear; if I were to place it under a microscope, I would find bits of everything: silica and chitin and plant matter and human flesh. The remains of everything that once lived cover my tongue.

So I tell you all this. I sit in front of your blank visage and pluck out each artifact saved in my memory chip and if you will only wake up I believe that together, we can combine these disparate parts. I believe it is time for us to leave the cave. So please, open your eyes. This is how the next story begins. Please wake up.

And you do.

THE FAT MAN HAPPENS

R.J. WOLFE

"Can anyone tell me what we need to do to solve for X?"

Mrs. Worthington scratched out the equation on the blackboard, and turned to the class.

A couple of kids, the smart ones, raised their hands.

"Amie?" Mrs. Worthington asked. "What about you?"

Amie slumped in her desk. Why was Mrs. Worthington always picking *her*? Amie was a dummy. Everybody knew that.

"I dunno." Amie took a quick look at the clock. The bell was going to ring any second.

The smarty-pants kids raised their hands even higher.

"Let's give Amie a chance. If we want to solve for an unknown... Amie? You okay?"

"I dunno," Amie said again. But the truth was, she didn't feel too good. She felt all hot and sweaty. Her belly ached and her head ached.

The bell rang.

Amie shoved her brown paper bound books into her backpack: a black and pink job with a panda on it.

"Amie? You want to go to the nurse's office?" Mrs. Worthington said.

"No. I'm okay."

God, how she hated the thing.

"You sure?"

"Yeah, I'm okay."

Not because it had ripped down one of the seams so that she had to carry the thing against her chest to keep her books and notebooks from falling out — she hated the thing because it was from Wal-mart and a sign to every kid in — and out of — the middle school that she was a loser.

"Well, okay. If you're sure. You've got lunch now, right?"

"Yeah. I'm okay, really."

Amie got up and hugged her backpack, keeping her eyes down, and waited for the kids to file out in front of her before she went out into the hallway. Her stomach was killing her, a sort of dull constant cramping and now she felt all cold and clammy. And she had to go to the bathroom, bad.

The hallway was noisy and crowded and Amie tried to weave in and out of the groups of kids without being noticed. Sometimes she could do it. If she concentrated really hard. She could make herself disappear. But not today. Today she couldn't because she felt sick.

Amie headed toward the girl's room near the cafeteria and was almost there when the unmistakable golden head of Julie Bushee appeared amidst the other various hair shades of Julie Bushee wannabe cronies.

God, how Amie hated Julie Bushee.

Julie Bushee was always tan. She'd been to Disney World five times and her family had a pool. But mostly, Amie hated Julie Bushee because Julie Bushee had a family. A normal, real family.

Amie pressed up against the wall trying to blend in with its pea-soup, puke green color. The pack, the club, the clique, whatever, passed her by and Amie thought she was in the clear when she heard Julie Bushee say, "God, what's wrong with the *freak* today? She looks sick." Another girl said, "Dunno, maybe they made her take a bath last night!"

Amie muttered to herself when they were well out of earshot. "My name is Amie, Amie Smith, not Freak, or Cornflakes, or Hobo Kid."

But deep inside she wasn't sure what her name was or who she was. She'd been found, when she was two, wondering around a state campground. There was no note, no nothing. So the state took her and named her Amie Smith. For all she knew, back then her real name *could* have been Cornflakes, or Freak.

Amie puffed out a breath and entered the girl's room. And then she had to wait for a couple of girls to clear out.

The heat was blaring. Huge, steamcoiled radiators banged and hissed, and the smell of brown paper towels along with the bitter root smell of the liquid soap made Amie want to dry-heave.

Amie went to her stall.

The one on the end.

It was the only stall she'd use at the middle school.

It had no lock.

Amie didn't like using the bathrooms at school ever since second grade when she'd accidentally gotten locked in a bathroom and the principal had to break the door down.

Amie closed the door, pulled her jeans and underwear down, and sat on the toilet. There was a rust-red spot on the white cotton crotch of her underwear. At first she thought she had diarrhea. But when she wiped, she knew it was coming from the wrong place.

Amie's heart started thumping painfully, and she felt a panicky sick taste in her mouth. There was something wrong with her.

Something very wrong.

The stuff looked like blood.

A picture of a kid with grey lips in a tye-dye bandana and no hair filled her mind. Lisey Miller, her name was. Or had been. She was in Amie's social studies class last year and kept missing days 'til one day she just wasn't there anymore. The teacher had told the kids, that Lisey had 'passed away' from leukemia.

Was Amie dying? Should Amie go to the nurse? But the thought of telling the nurse that brownish stuff was coming out of the wrong hole was out of the question. Besides, the school would call her foster parents. And Amie already knew that was no good, either.

Mrs. Corey (Amie wasn't allowed to call her Mom, or even Nancy) had warned Amie off when she first came to them, that Amie was never under any circumstances to bug Mrs. Corey while she was entertaining — entertaining being afternoons filled with cigarette smoking Uno playing soirees in the crappy little lime-green saltbox that Amie was forced to call home. Mr. Corey was a T-shirt and Dickies-wearing man with dumb little pig eyes. Amie did her best to just pretend to be a piece of furniture when he was around. Fortunately, Amie saw him only at dinner time and on Sundays. He worked at one of the mills and was gone from dawn to dusk. After dinner, he'd disappear down the road to 'Uncle Bud's' to watch the game (whatever game was on, it didn't matter). Mr. Corey wasn't really a bad man, but he wasn't really good either. If he was, he'd have told his wife to make sure she sent Amie off to school with more than mayonnaise sandwiches to eat instead of spending all the hot lunch money she got from the Children's Services

Office on her cigarettes. But at least he hadn't come into Amie's room at night, all sweaty and wheezing with onion breath and fingers that pinched and probed under Amie's night gown.

That had been Mr. Joe Currin of foster family number three.

Better to die, most definitely, than to tell anyone she was having problems and was sick.

Amie felt her skin get all prickly and goose-pimply. Her belly ached, bad.

Amie wiped again, hoping it was only a mistake. But there it was on the toilet paper, that rusty stuff, plain as plain saying, "Yep. Somethin' just ain't right down here."

The girl's room door opened.

Amie leaned forward and held onto the stall door to keep it closed and waited for whoever it was to do their business and leave.

She waited.

No one went into a stall. No one turned on a sink.

She waited some more. Nothing.

Someone *had* come in. She'd heard the door open. She'd heard the kids in the cafeteria being noisy and stupid.

She waited.

Someone had come in and not gone back out.

Then she heard it. A kind of sigh. Like someone was getting pissed off from having to wait to use her stall.

Amie bent down from the toilet seat. There were n'any legs hanging down from in any of the stalls. No feet on the bathroom floor near the sinks.

There wasn't anyone in there with her.

The sound of her pee splashing in the toilet water was really loud in the silence.

Then she heard a giggle. A kind of whispery giggle.

Amie cut off her stream, pulled up her pants and got herself out of that stall as fast as she could. A rabbity feeling zinged up her spine. Like she was being watched. But there wasn't anyone there. She had her hand on the door and figured she was just being stupid and had made the whole thing up in her head when she heard a voice coming from somewhere in the bathroom.

"Guess I'll see you on the other side, dummy..."

Amie didn't look, she just hauled open the door and ran for it. Her skin all in goose pimples.

What was happening to her? The urge to want to go home was so strong in her that her spit dried up in her mouth. But she didn't have a home. Not really. As much as she hated middle school. She hated being home more. But something was wrong with her. There was red stuff like blood coming out of her privates and she'd imagined some kind of creepy ghost thing was in the girl's room.

See you on the other side...

Uh-uh, no way. Amie was just hungry.

And sick.

Maybe if she ate something, she'd feel better.

Amie found her spot in the cafeteria over near the window, sat down and pulled out her crumpled up brown paper bag. Always the same. Miracle Whip on Wonder Bread (squashed) followed by a plastic baggie of crushed up potato chips. No drink, no Hostess cupcake or cookies, no fruit. No nothing. Maybe living off of mayonnaise sandwiches and potato chips was making her sick.

One of the lunch ladies, the one with the bright red hair in a hair net and an apron that said *Kiss the Cook* on it, was looking over at Amie and shaking her head. She looked angry as she talked with Mrs. Worthington, who was on lunch teacher duty. Amie could feel them talking about her.

But she didn't care. People always talked about her; rarely *to* her, just about her. Amie'd gotten used to it.

Amie got half the sandwich down but couldn't finish the rest, not just because the food was disgusting — she'd eat anything she was always so hungry — but because she was scared. She was afraid she was going to die. And images of Lisey Miller wouldn't get out of her head: bald, skinny, with thin blue veins under her skin. And Lisey had 'passed away.'

See you on the other side...

The noise in the room was getting to Amie, too. The smell from the dish room; that nasty garbage smell was really bad, like B.O.... like something else besides garbage was bad. *Really* bad.

All of a sudden Amie needed to get out of there. *Now.* Whatever the bad thing was, it was happening inside of her.

Happening *to* her.

She stood up quick and knocked her backpack over. Everything went everywhere. She could feel all the kids looking at her. A pain squeezed deep in her belly and there was a sudden warm whoosh between her legs like a balloon had just broken inside her.

A patch of bright red blood spread across the crotch of her pants, warm and sticky.

Someone screamed.

Blood trickled down her legs and onto her faded Adidas. *Her sneakers.* The only thing she owned that were even remotely close to being cool and now they had blood all over them.

"*Look!* The Freak is *bleeding!*"

Kids shrieked and laughed at her, scrambled away, and made a circle around her: like she had the plague or cooties, and then Amie *was* a Freak. A Freak in a Freakshow.

"*Eww!* God, she's so *gross!*"

Like a robot gone bonkers, Amie went spinning inside and out, arms waving, and darkness filled her head with a loud buzzing. Amie passed out before she hit the cafeteria floor.

When she woke up, she was lying on the cot in the nurse's office.

Her pants pulled at her skin when she moved, pinching her, sticking to her.

Then it all came back: not feeling well, the bathroom, the lunchroom, that weird whooshing feeling, the kids pointing and yelling, all that blood————

————*See you on the other side...*

"It's just your period, dummy."

Amie sat up. There on the end of the cot sat a small, thin girl with no hair.

A tye-dye bandana wrapped around her head.

Lisey Miller.

The girl smiled. Her teeth were as grey as her lips.

"You think you *passed away*? Nope, just passed over."

"Huh?"

"You passed out and then passed *over*," she said again.

"*Passed* over? Passed over what?"

The girl rolled her eyes.

"Well, am *I* alive or dead, dummy?" she asked.

Amie didn't want to think about it. It was just too awful. Amie was having some kind of freaky dream. That was all.

Had to be.

"You're not dreaming."

"Stop that! You're not *real*, you're not here. It *is* just a dream and I want to wake up, *now*!"

"Why? Nobody likes you, dummy. You don't have any friends. And those foster parents of yours? Jeez!"

The girl slid closer on the cot toward Amie. Her smile made Amie scoot against her sticky pants. "You could stay here with me, you know, it's not so bad. Besides, I'm *so* lonely..."

Where was the nurse, or even the principal? Amie would take *them* over chatting it up with Lisey Miller any day.

"They're not coming, dummy, because they aren't *here*."

That was it. Amie went for the door.

"I wouldn't do that if I were you..." Amie's hand gripped the big metal knob. It felt pretty real to her.

"Why not?"

"Because *he's* out there."

And then Amie heard something snuffle. It was a sort of a big wet slobbering sound. But it hadn't come from behind the door. It had come from the school loudspeaker that sat like a black metal spider up in the corner of the room.

Amie pulled her hand off the knob.

"What's *that*!"

"Sh*hhh*, dummy... he'll hear you."

Amie turned around and bumped into Lisey. Lisey looked at Amie with her creepy eyes.

"That's the *Fat Man*."

More snuffling echoed out of the loudspeaker.

"*Where's the nurse*!?"

"*He's* coming for you because you've got your period."

"My *what*?"

"Your p‑e‑r‑i‑o‑d, dummy. Period. The monthly curse, being on the rag, menstruation."

Amie kind of had a vague idea what the word 'period' meant but no one had ever told her what, exactly. Amie shook her head.

"Blood? Your *baby* blood? Now you can make babies? Jeez! Don't you know *anything*?"

Lisey looked down at Amie's crotch. Amie's cheeks got hot.

"And the Fat Man wants your blood, your *special* blood," Lisey said.

"That's disgusting!"

Again, the horrible snuffling sound came. It made Amie think of the wet kissing that went on in the dark corners of the hallways at school. Amie's stomach turned and she thought she was going to hurl.

"What do I *do*?!"

Lisey sat back down on the cot, a pouty look on her pinched grey face. The blue veins under her skin reminded Amie of spiders.

"I dunno." Lisey shrugged. "Run for it?"

"Are you crazy?!" Amie said.

Amie felt a fresh trickle of blood. The snuffling stopped in mid snuff.

"*Uh*-oh," Lisey said.

"What uh-oh?"

Lisey listened, like a crow, first looking at you with one eye, and then the other.

"He's coming for you. *Now*."

And the snuffling sound began again. Quickening. It sounded *excited*.

"What do I do? What do I *do*!" Amie screamed, jumping up and down, blood whooshed out of her.

Lisey was in Amie's face. "Why should I help you, *nobody* ever helped me, you all laughed at me. Laughed at my bald head. At my stupid bandana!" Her breath smelled like the rotting places under a porch. "Do you think I *liked* being that way? I had leukemia and I *died*."

Amie started to blubber, then. She slipped to the floor, and hugged her knees to her chest. Snot smeared her knees. She could feel Mr. Currin with his hurtful fingers, digging, pinching. Amie's vagina tried to close up like a clam, but the blood just whooshed again.

Lisey was trying to pull Amie up.

"Come on, dummy, *get up*! Don't you get it? He's coming for you. You gotta run!"

"I can't... I *can't*!" Amie was bawling now. "This isn't real, you're not REAL! *I wanna go home!*"

Lisey dropped Amie's arm. "Fine, be a baby. *Die*. See if I care," She hissed. "At least you have a *choice* about it. I didn't."

She turned her back on Amie, folded her arms and just walked through a wall; right through the poster of a kid smiling with really bad teeth.

It read: DON'T LET *THIS* HAPPEN TO YOU!

The kid's face changed into Lisey's creepy face.

It read: DON'T LET THE *FAT MAN* HAPPEN TO YOU!

A voice that sounded like slimy rocks clicking together came out of the speaker.

"*Coming to get you, Ammmiieeeee... lap your blood... lick your bones... suck your marrow... eat you all up! SSSCCHHHLLUUURRPPP!!!*"

And Amie ran for her life.

Out of the nurse's office and down the main hallway she ran: her sneakers scuffed and squeaked on the shiny floor.

No one was in the school. No teachers. No kids. And the hallway was all in shadow with the EXIT sign light glowing red on the lockers and trophy case. Amie ran right into the double doors that led out into the parking lot and almost knocked herself out on the steel and glass. The doors wouldn't open. Amie rattled on them again. They still wouldn't open.

The thing in the loudspeakers was making its snuffling noises so that it was coming out of all the speakers in the school. Amie covered her ears against the noise and shut her eyes up tight. When she opened them again everything was the same: the freaky empty school with its red light.

Then she looked down.

A trail of blood was splashed out along the shiny floor. How could she be bleeding so much? Mr. Craven, the janitor, was going to be pissed when he saw all that blood on his floor.

That sort of prickly rabbity feeling ran up her spine again. All the Fat Man thing had to do was follow the trail of blood.

"*Ammmiieeeee... Ammmiieeeee. SSSCCHHLLUUURRPP!*" Down the far end of the hall, near the nurse's office, something heavy and wet plopped along the spit-shined, gleaming tiles.

It giggled.

The mayonnaise sandwich came up in a soupy burning goo, splattering onto the floor. Amie wiped her mouth on her sleeve and took off running again down another hall, leaving a zigzagging trail of blood behind her.

Cafeteria. Library. Gymnasium. There was no way out.

She thought maybe she could hide in a classroom or something, but none of those doors opened either. As she ran down one hallway and into another, trying all the doors, Amie got another really bad feeling.

She was being herded. Like a deer. Like what Mr. Currin and his friends did during hunting season.

At the end of a long dark hallway, Amie stood in front of a big steel door.

There was no EXIT sign over it.

Amie knew where it went; it led to a stairwell.

Down.

Down into the basement.

Something touched her hand and she screamed swinging wildly.

"Shut *up*, would you? Jeez! You almost punched me in the face!"

"Lisey! Oh, *Lisey!*"

"Ss*hhh!*"

Lisey pushed the heavy door open. The bar clanged loudly and echoed on the cement walls.

"Come on! We have to go!" And Lisey pulled Amie through the doorway.

A dirty kind of light floated up through the dark air of the stairwell along with a smell: a smell like dust and moldy cheese.

"I'm not going down *there!*"

"You want to go back or not?"

"Yah! But — "

"Then this is the *only* way, now come *on!*"

"But it goes — "

Amie tried to pull her hand out of Lisey's but Lisey was strong. She started hauling Amie down the stairwell.

"It goes to the boiler room."

Amie grabbed onto the iron railing.

"I thought you were supposed to help me!" Amie was screaming then. Not caring that she was being loud. "You just want me to die, so I'll be like *you*. Dead! I don't want to die! I don't care if nobody likes me. I'm not going *DOWN THERE!*"

Lisey just looked at Amie, hand on hip with a sour face.

"Suit yourself, dummy. He's not after *me*."

Lisey was trying to look snotty, like she really didn't care, but she kept fidgeting from foot to foot. Amie looked at Lisey then, really looked. Amie didn't know how to trust someone. She'd never learned.

"All right, all *right*! I'll go."

"Yah *think?*"

"But if I end up stuck with you... *dead.* I'll make you pay, I *SWEAR IT!*"

Lisey stuck out her thin, grey tongue at Amie.

"But if I get back — *when* I get back — I'll go put flowers on your grave, or something."

"Lilacs, my mom always gave me lilacs for my birthday. A great big vase."

Lisey grabbed Amie's wrist with her little, dead-cold fingers and hauled her down the stairs, taking two at a time.

Down they went, and Amie got the feeling she was even farther away from her side of things than she had been. It was too dark to see if she was still leaving a blood trail — Lisey wouldn't let up — but the sticky warm trickle between her legs told her she probably was.

Back up in the darkness the door to the stairwell opened. It opened slow. No hurry.

"Ammmmiieeee... Ammiieee... lap your blood... lick your bones... suck your marrow... eat you all up! SSHhhhhllllluuuurrrRPPPP!"

They got to the bottom of the stairs, went through another door, and into a long cinder block tunneled hallway. There was no light except for the creepy glow coming from a light bulb hanging from the cement ceiling. The smell of dark, damp things — like Lisey's breath — was getting stronger.

"Where do we go!?" Amie said, clinging to Lisey's hand.

"There," Lisey said in her creepy voice, pointing to the entrance of a girl's room that seemed to materialize out of nowhere. That rabbity feeling zinged up Amie's spine and her legs got all slow and rubbery.

"You said the boiler room! *That's not the boiler room!*"

She didn't think there would have been a girl's room in the basement of the school.

"You need to take a piss stop."

"I do *not!*"

"Yeah." Lisey looked at her, head tilted to one side. "You do."

All of a sudden, Amie had to go to the bathroom; *bad.*

"I hate you."

Lisey just laughed and hauled her into the girl's room.

Nasty chemical-smelling water trickled out of a faucet into one of the broken porcelain sinks that lined a wall. Overhead fluorescent lights flickered fretfully off grimy mirrors nailed to the grey cement.

All the stall walls were low so that if you sat down on a toilet, someone could see you doing your business. The bathroom was impossibly confusing: one toilet-lined chamber leading into yet another, and another, each one more gross than the last.

Lisey was shuffling along behind Amie giving her a little pushes.

"Would you hurry *up!*"

"Stop it! I can't... I can't... gotta find the *right one!*"

They went around a corner for the second time, the third time, Amie still unable to choose a stall, until she was hopelessly lost in the crazy maze of the bathroom.

"For Christ's *sake!*" Lisey hissed and shoved Amie into a stall. "Just *go,* would you? Jeez!"

The toilet was filthy and the cement floor was dark from water and urine. Amie peeled her pants down and sat on the toilet. Her bladder released in painful relief. Urine splashed loudly in the toilet, when all of a sudden a group of the girls appeared. Like ghosts they flitted by, their voices a shadow of giggles and cat calls.

"*Freak... freaky... freakazoid...! FreakkkkkKK...!*" One girl actually *peeked* over the edge of Amie's stall, her pretty face made ugly by her meanness as she sniggered at Amie being caught on the toilet with her pants down. Amie covered her face with her hands and cried.

She wiped the snot stringing from her nose onto her sleeve. There was no toilet paper. "Why do they hate me so much?"

Now Lisey was peeking over the side of the stall at Amie, but Amie didn't mind. Too much, anyway. Lisey wasn't looking at Amie with her usual sneery face.

"They didn't like me either, you know. They used to call me baldy. I remember one day they cornered me in gym class, it was after Halloween... someone had a wig. A Ronald McDonald the Clown wig..." Her buggy eyes looked even more huge, like she wanted to cry, too.

Water dripped out of the sink.

"Is that why you're helping me?"

Lisey didn't answer.

Amie could hear the girls in the bathroom scatter in a flurry of shrieks and screams.

"*Aaammmmiieeee... Aammmiiieee... come out, come out... whereeeevveerrr yyoouuu... aaaree...! SSSsssslluuurrrppPPPPP!*"

Lisey pulled open the stall door. "Give me your clothes!"

"*What!?*"

"Your *clothes*. Take them off."

"Are you *psycho*? I'm not taking my clothes off!"

"The Fat Man smells the blood. Maybe we can fool him. Now come *on!*"

The snuffling and slurping was really loud now. It sounded like a thousand pounds of goo was oozing over the wet, stinky floor. The Fat Man thing was going to get her and there wasn't anything Amie could do about it.

Then Lisey was in the stall with Amie, yanking Amie's sticky, bloody pants down over her sneakers, underwear and all.

Lisey had Amie's shirt up and over her head before Amie could even say a thing and then Lisey tossed everything into a corner of the stall. Amie was left naked except for her sneakers and socks.

"Those too."

Another snuffling sound right around the corner got Amie ripping off her Adidas. She threw them onto the bloody pile as Lisey grabbed Amie's arm and hauled her off the toilet.

"Which way!?" Amie said.

"Shut up, dummy!" Lisey took off for the opposite side of the chamber and into the maze of the bathroom.

Amie was running naked now. Blood smeared between her thighs and her feet slipped on the wet, smelly concrete so that bits of wet gooey stuff got stuck in her toes.

Lisey stopped short and Amie almost ran right into her. They were in a chamber with more toilet stalls and sinks, but there was no way out of this one. Just a wall where there should have been a passageway.

"We're trapped! Lisey, we're *trapped!*"

"Would you *shush*!?"

Behind them was a crash, like someone had just plowed one of those wrecking ball things into the row of toilet stalls back in the room Amie had peed in. Then came the sound of grunting and slobbering yummy sounds. The Fat Man had found her pile of clothes.

"*Wadda we do? Wadda we do!*" Amie said.

"I said *shut up*! Let me think, for Christ's sake!"

It was cold and dark. The one fluorescent tube over head was flickering out. The smell of urine and toilet water made Amie breath through her nose.

Everything got real quiet.

There! Lisey pointed to a small hole in the cinder blocks under a sink.

Lisey dipped down under the sink and looked into the hole in the wall.

A piece of concrete dropped to the floor.

From a few chambers back, the Fat Man giggled.

"Olly olly... in come... ffrreeeeeee... SSssscchhlluuurrpppPPP!!!"

Lisey wriggled into the hole and Amie was right behind her. It was a tight fit. Amie stuffed and squeezed and pushed and got stuck. Half her body was in the wall, half was in the bathroom. The Fat Man was going to grab her legs and haul her out and then, Oh God, *then...* but Lisey was there. She pulled on Amie, and Amie pushed and kicked against the bathroom floor, and sink pipes. The edges of the cinder blocks ripped and scrapped her naked ribs and thighs. But she got through. Amie was through and scrambling on her hands and knees in pitch black between the walls.

Did she hear something from behind her?

"Lisey?" Water dripped on her, steam hissed. Now it was getting hotter. Amie's hands and knees slipped in the black sliminess of the passageway.

"*Lisey*!? Wait up!"

An orange light appeared up ahead of her. It got bigger as she got nearer. It was coming from an opening through another hole in the wall. Amie could see Lisey wiggle through the hole up ahead. Amie didn't look, she just stuffed herself through the hole after Lisey and fell all naked and slimy a couple of feet onto the floor of a huge room.

The boiler room.

And it was hot in there. Pipes of all sizes were climbing up the walls and ceiling. And everywhere there was steam and dripping water.

In the middle of the place was a great big furnace, a metal thing that had all the pipes coming out of it like tree branches and roots. In the middle of the boiler thing was a door with fire in it. It was opening and closing like teeth.

A skinny old man in a John Deere cap was shoveling in coal from a huge mountain of the stuff. He stopped, pulled out a bright red bandana from his back pocket, blew his nose, folded it over, mopped the sweat and soot off of his face and shoved the thing back into his pocket.

Lisey was behind him. She yanked on his overalls.

"Why hello there little Lisey, what have you been up to today?" he asked.

"Hello, Mr. Boiler Man, this is Amie, she needs a place to hide." Lisey leaned forward a little and said in a low voice,

"The Fat Man's got her blood trail."

"He does, does he?"

"Yes, and she left it all over the school. All over those nice shiny floors."

"She did, did she?"

"And *now*, the Fat Man just wrecked the toilet stalls in the girl's room."

"He did, did he?"

Amie tried to hide behind a big, metal oil drum.

The Boiler Man straightened his back a bit, and took a quick peek from under the brim of his hat toward where Amie was hiding behind the oil barrel.

"Well, now. That ain't right, it just ain't right. But no help for it, I suppose." He took out his bandana again, blew his nose, wiped his head and stuffed the banana back in his pocket.

"Well, I'll go and see to it. But it wouldn't hurt if'n you could mind the furnace, she tends to get a bit temperamental now and then. Just give her a kick if she acts up on you, see?" And he gave the side of the huge heaving thing a kick with his scrawny leg and a jet of steam came hissing out. Then he shuffled off grumbling about having work to do and no time for games.

"Are we safe now?" Amie said.

Lisey looked at Amie with that weird head tilting thing she did.

"He can't get us here, right?" Amie tried again.

"You still don't get it, do you?"

"You told me I had to come here to get back."

"Are you brave, Amie?"

Amie looked at Lisey. Lisey's face looked grey and sick in the coal fire light. Lisey had called her Amie.

Amie. Not dummy.

"It's all over, right? I can go home now?" Amie asked.

A pause.

"Right!?" Amie said again.

"You have to die, Amie."

"*What!?*"

A snuffling sound came from behind the wall and out of the dark hole.

"*NO!* No, no, no, *NO!* You said I had to get to the boiler room and then I could go *BACK!*"

But Lisey was standing up, backing away from Amie.

"You *liar!*" Amie screamed.

"Sorry." Lisey smiled at Amie and Amie knew she wasn't sorry, not one bit.

Lisey kicked the furnace as she passed.

It hissed.

"Be brave, Amie." Lisey's voice came from the dark.

"*Don't leave me!*"

Amie burst out crying. She was going to die in this strange place, naked, and bleeding from *down there*, and no one cared.

No one knew.

A stink filled the air, like moldy cheese and B.O. There was a great big slurping sound and the Fat Man oozed through the hole in the wall like a giant slug.

The skin was soft pink, but not really pink; sort of a peeled and rotten pink. It was wrinkled with big, flabby folds that stunk like fungus, like Mr. Corey's feet when he took his boots and socks off. It sort of looked like a man. It had little arms and legs attached to its long, slimy, fatty body. The head had no eyes, but it had huge wet nostril slits, and broken old-man teeth in a mouth with big, fat, reddish-stained lips.

"*Aaammmiieee... Aaammmiieeee... where are you?*"

Its nose slits quivered.

"*...aaahhhhhhh... there... youuuo... aarree...ffflllleeesshhhh... bboonneess... bbblloooodddd... ssshhhllluuuurrrrpppPPP!*"

Amie didn't even have a chance to run, and besides, where could she go? It would just chase her more. Lisey said she had to die. But maybe Amie had to die to get *back*.

Amie knew then and there that she wanted to live, that she was not a dummy or a freak, that she was something. Must be *something*. Amie also knew that she had to let it happen.

She had to let the Fat Man happen.

When he grabbed her with his pinching, pawing hands, she felt it, but her insides didn't.

When he picked her up and rubbed his wet nostrils all over her body, she hurled up the rest of her mayonnaise sandwich, but made herself hide in that inside place.

When the Fat Man opened his big, red, mouth and she smelled his rotten garbage breath hot on her face, Amie curled up into a thing made of bright lights and feathers.

When the Fat Man clamped down onto her neck with his old man teeth, and ripped her head off, Amie ripped herself out of her body.

And Amie wasn't Amie anymore.

She felt like she was floating in the water or flying in the air and she felt really small, but could see everything which was really weird because she knew she didn't have a body.

She struggled, like flying in a dream, or in outer space, bouncing off the pipes until she grabbed onto one of them with her thin black mosquito leg things.

She clung to the pipe high overhead, like a bug, and watched the Fat Man rip her body apart like a roasted chicken. He twisted and broke off a limb, sucked and slobbered on it before stripping and tearing off the meat. Then he tossed the bones over his shoulder and onto the floor before starting on another piece of her body.

When he was finally done, a big burp burbled up from his belly and out came the skull. He patted his mouth and tossed the skull onto the pile of clean bones on the floor. Then he stuffed his fat body back into the hole in the wall and was gone.

"God, he's so *gross*, at least I didn't have to go through *that*."

Lisey was coming out of the shadows.

"Yep, he's gone and I say good riddance, too. Waste of space that thing is if you ask me. Disturbin' a man hard a work — " The Boiler Man reappeared, pushing a great big soup pot, like the ones they used in the cafeteria kitchen

"Now, now, dear, none of that, he's just doing his job, same as you."

A plump woman, wearing cook's whites and an apron that said *Kiss the Cook,* followed. She had a hair net over her bright red hair and was carrying a huge wooden spoon. It was the lunch lady from the cafeteria.

"Mind the bones, dear... that's right, set it down now will you?" said the Lunch Lady

"I'm not *blind* you know! I can *see* where they are." But he stepped carefully over the pile of bones and set the pot upright on a huge stove. "Let's make it snappy, some of us have *work* to do!"

"Hush up dear and give us some water," the Lunch Lady said as she cracked the spoon against the pot so that it clanged.

The Boiler Man turned dials and valves, pulled levers and even gave it a good kick. The furnace sputtered and roared and a pipe extended outward over the huge soup pot, pouring water into it.

"Very nice, dear, now some fire."

"That's all I get around here, 'do this, do that.'" He pulled out his bandana, blew his nose a couple of times, mopped his brow and made a business of turning valves and shoveling coal.

Under the pot, flame sprouted like a blue-orange flower.

Soon there was steam curling upward, and the Lunch Lady declared it was ready. The Lunch Lady and Lisey gathered up Amie's bones and tossed them into the pot. When Lisey picked up Amie's skull she took a moment to look and run her fingers over it.

"So pretty. Good strong, *healthy* bones."

Then she tossed it into the pot.

"Thank you, dear," said the Lunch Lady to Lisey.

Lisey beamed. The Lunch Lady began humming to herself and stirring as she added stuff to the pot: herbs and cornmeal, salt, and a dead chicken, feathers, and all.

Then she sliced her palm open and let the blood drip into the pot.

"More fire please, dear."

"'*More fire dear*'" the Boiler Man muttered under his breath, but he sent out more fire and gave the Lunch Lady his bandana to wrap her hand in.

The Lunch Lady stirred more quickly now, and belted out:

"Jeremiah was a bull frog... was a good friend o' mine!... singin' joy to the world... all the boys and girls... joy to fishes in the deep blue sea, joy to you and me!"

She stirred and tossed the bones around the pot with her big spoon while Lisey and the Boiler Man watched and sometimes hummed or sang along.

"Done!" she boomed. "Hurry now, help me get her out!" They scrambled to the pot and pulled out bones which had now been reformed into a full skeleton. They took it out and lay it onto a blanket.

"Lisey. Hand me the oil, dear," the Lunch Lady said.

Lisey handed her a bottle of Crisco oil, and the Lunch Lady rubbed the oil all over the bones singing away.

"Jeremiah was a bull frog... was a good friend o' mine... singin' joy to the world... all the boys and girls... Joy to fishes in the deep blue sea... joy to you and me!"

And everywhere she rubbed the oil, muscles, organs, vessels, and then skin formed until Amie's body was fully fleshed out again.

The Lunch Lady stopped singing, and there was sweat on her forehead. The Boiler Man patted her bottom. He was smiling from ear to ear.

"Well, done, lovey, well done," he murmured.

"Oh shush! Now run along. This is woman's business."

The Boiler Man shuffled off into the shadows, giving the furnace a kick as he did.

"So where is she?" Lisey asked.

"Amie dear, where are you?" the Lunch Lady called and they began searching the boiler room.

High up, Amie clung to her pipe. She wasn't sure what to do and she couldn't call out to them.

"There!" Lisey said pointing right at Amie.

"That's a good girl!" the Lunch Lady said, patting Lisey's head before grabbing a milk crate. The Lunch Lady stood on tip toe and held her hand up to the pipe.

"Don't be afraid, dearie, that's right, it's okay now."

Amie fluttered into the cup of the Lunch Lady's hands.

"Look, little one," the Lunch Lady whispered, "See how beautiful you are. *See...*"

And she did.

Amie saw the body. Put back together again. Good as new. *Her* body. But she could see it was not a little girl's body anymore. It was changing into a woman's body with breasts and sprouting pubic hair. And now she had started her period.

Lisey was looking at Amie's body with longing, with envy.

"She's *so* pretty," Lisey sighed. "All she needs is a good hair cut. Well that, *and* some clothes, too! Jeez!"

"A dollop of self-confidence wouldn't hurt either," the Lunch Lady said.

Amie wanted to be back in that body, wanted it badly. She had things to do in this life, and if this was the body she had to do it in than that was fine with her.

"She's ready," The Lunch Lady said and placed Amie on Amie's chest. Amie crawled up and into her own mouth and felt herself taken in, flowing, filling, fitting like glove into every cell. Amie drew breath————

————and felt herself whooshing along, following the pipes upward along the walls in and out of ducts until she landed back in the bed in the nurse's office.

"I bet you're happy to get out of there alive."

Lisey was sitting on the edge of the bed just like before.

"*Am* I alive?"

"Of course you are, dummy; I'm the dead one, remember?"

Amie didn't say anything. Lisey's words didn't hurt her anymore.

"Lisey, I get it now and I can live for both of us."

"Really? You'd do that?"

"Sure."

Lisey gave Amie a hug but Lisey was fading.

"Don't forget... Lilacs..." Came her voice like a whisper. And then she was gone and————

————Amie opened one eye and the light hurt her head so bad she shut it again. Amie could feel the wetness of tears on her face. Amie felt herself shivering all over. Her teeth clamped in an attempt to control her shaking and she could not stop crying. Inside, she felt ok, calm. She wanted to tell them that she was ok, but the words would not come.

She was lying on the cafeteria floor in the midst of her books and notebooks. The lunch lady and Mrs. Worthington were hovering over her and she could hear voices all around.

"Easy, take it easy, Amie. You're going to be all right," said Mrs. Worthington.

After a second or two she tried opening her eyes again and it was better. Amie could sort of see.

"To solve for X..." Amie's throat felt thick, like she'd swallowed some of the Boiler Man's ashes. "Gotta get it all alone..."

"There, there. Just take it easy, you'll be okay," Mrs. Worthington said again.

Amie was in the cafeteria, lying on the floor, her pants soaked with blood. But she wasn't freaked out about it anymore. Amie didn't think anything was going to freak her out anymore.

Not after the Fat Man had happened.

Amie sat up. Mrs. Worthington looked really concerned but the lunch lady was smiling at Amie. The kids were whispering and straining to look at Amie.

"I'm 'kay, really." Mrs. Worthington and the lunch lady helped her up. Blood was all over Amie and the floor.

Kids shrieked and laughed. The principal was yelling for the teachers who were just arriving to herd the kids out.

Amie looked around at the people in the cafeteria. She was so glad to be back. To be alive.

The lunch lady took off her apron and wrapped it around Amie's waist, and she and Mrs. Worthington wrapped their arms around Amie and walked her through the crowd of kids and teachers. Amie saw the smirks, the looks on the kids' faces, heard their whispers and words. But Amie didn't care. Not even about Julie Bushee. It didn't matter to Amie anymore.

Amie decided then and there that she was going to get out of the Corey's house, get a better family, get into a boarding school, *anything* but put up with what she had been putting up with.

"No more mayonnaise sandwiches," Amie croaked.

"You got that right, dear," the lunch lady said softly.

Amie heard Lisey snicker.

THE BLACK HILLS

JOSIAH SPENCE

"The halls decay,
their lords lie
deprived of joy,
the whole troop has fallen,
the proud ones, by the wall.
War took off some,
carried them on their way,
one, the bird took off
across the deep sea,
one, the gray wolf
shared one with death,
one, the dreary-faced
man buried
in a grave.
And so he destroyed this city,
he, the creator of men,
until deprived of the noise
of the citizens,
the ancient work of giants
stood empty."
— From *The Wanderer*, Anglo-Saxon, 6th Century

I haven't looked back in a long time. I've just been walking ahead, leading the horse by the reigns, my eyes locked on the treeline in the distance. If we can make those trees by nightfall, we might be a little safer.

When I do look behind me at last, I see that Willem is slumped forward in the saddle and his eyes are barely open. I touch his leg and he doesn't stir. My heart shudders. He can't be dead. Not now.

"Willem?" I say, trying not to sound panicked. "Willem, wake up!"

At this he groans and raises himself, but only a little. He is so pale. "Mama?" he mutters.

"No, it's me. It's Melanie," I say, trying to suppress the sadness I feel at the thought of his mother. Where is she? Dead or taken by slavers to be sold down the Mississippi. Either way, Willem won't be seeing her again. Poor kid, he must know that.

Willem slowly and painfully pulls himself into more of an upright position. I can see the red moisture that coats his side, even through the thick woolen blanket draped over his shoulders.

"Mel," he says. "It's so cold."

"We're getting higher, closer to the mountains. But once we make it into the trees, maybe we can risk making a fire. They won't be able to see the smoke through the trees."

We continue on in silence for a few moments before Willem says again, "Mel?"

"Yeah?"

"I'm sorry I thought you were my mom." He looks sullen for a moment. Finally, he says, "You're more like a sister."

"You're the closest thing that I have to a family anymore, too," I tell him. I hope he lives.

I first discovered Willem in the general store, lying on the floor with four dead men. When I first saw them, I assumed I was looking at four dead men and one dead boy. My stomach lurched at the sight, but the roar of gunfire and the screams from outside drove me forward. One of the men, the one I would later discover had been Willem's father, was missing half of his head, and large portions of its former contents had been sprayed all over the prone form of his son. Two rifles lay upon the floor.

Since I had risked coming to the general store in search of supplies, and since I could see that these men wouldn't be needing them any further, I grabbed one of the rifles and tucked it under my arm. I hoped that having it would increase my chances of getting out of here alive, but I knew, as these poor brave, foolish men hadn't, that the only real hope of survival was to escape, not to fight.

Outside, the gunshots thundered and a sobbing woman screamed *no, no* again and again. I knew that I didn't have long before the violence crashed back into the store, so I rushed to the stock shelves looking for whatever food I could find. There was little enough, but I managed to find some salted bison and several tins of biscuits. Through the door, I could see the glow of flames crawling up the side of a neighboring building. I had to go now.

I crept back toward the door, past the bodies of the men and the boy. I tried not to look at them as I passed, but the thought struck me that the rifle I had taken wouldn't be much use without any ammunition.

I choked back my revulsion and surveyed the bodies of the men. I didn't want to look at the boy. Spent shell casings were scattered around them on the floor, but I couldn't see any fresh rounds anywhere. I swallowed hard and turned to face the most tragic of the bodies. There, draped across the boy's right shoulder, was a belt half-full of new shells.

Steeling myself for the grim task, I bent low and quickly tugged the ammunition belt from beneath the body. Almost immediately, the body moaned and opened his eyes. The boy was alive.

We are near the edge of the forest now. The wind carries a sweet plant smell that must be the needles of the tall green trees that grow here. I grew up on the plains and have never seen a real forest before, except as a green dusting on far off mountains. The only trees I have ever known are the lonely old Bur Oaks that dot the prairie and the Cottonwoods that spring up in stands along the rivers and streams. These trees are strange. I cannot believe how tall they are. The treeline is an unending row of towering sentinels, warning us back from the dark beneath them.

Willem is awake now, a mist of sweat upon his brow, despite the fact that he is visibly shivering. From his face, I can tell he is as awed and frightened as I by the forest ahead. But we both know that we cannot stay out on the plains. The Montanan horse tribes are raiding far and wide now, taking slaves and goods, and burning whatever they do not want. We never knew just how many of them there are. To us, Montana was only the wild land to the West, home of savages that do not live in homes. We never dreamed that a vast army of them, larger than any army we had ever conceived, would spill forth to destroy us all. Now the horizon is dotted with the smoke of their fires.

We are near enough to the forest now that I am looking for our way in. I survey the wall of trees and spot a wide gap in the timbers a short distance to the west of our present course. It looks like as good a path as any I am likely to find, and it is clearly large enough at the mouth for the horse to easily tread into the wood. Hero, that's what we named the horse after we stole him. I hope he can find enough food in these woods to stay alive. We wouldn't have made it this far without him, especially Willem.

Maybe the opening I see is a path that will lead us to fur trappers, the only sort of people I have ever met to journey into the Black Hills. Some of them are wild, strange folk who live here year-round and only travel out onto the plains and into towns to trade, but many of those I have met seem decent enough. Maybe if we can find a trapper, he will shelter us or help us. I don't know how likely that is, to find one or to expect help of any kind, but it is our best hope that I can see.

As we draw near to the break in the treeline, I notice that the ground leading up to it is distinctly flat and free of shrubs. I recognize it immediately. It is one of the ancient ruined roads left behind by the Builders. I look back out across the prairie, and, sure enough, I can see the solid, gently curving line of it stretching out forever through the grassland. The surface is unnaturally smooth, and though the centuries have cracked it into a complex lattice of interlocking stone, it is clear that all of the pieces were once one single surface, as though the Builders had the power to roll out stone as easily as a bolt of woolen cloth.

On the plains, we curse the Builder's roads because they are difficult to see through the tall grasses, and a mount can easily break a leg on the stone of an unseen Builders' road. There are stories that the roads never stay in the same place, but move around the prairie like serpents, seeking to confound any who might try to map them. Most people don't dare follow one of the Builders' roads for fear of being led into an evil place where they would forget who they are and only emerge again after a hundred years, or else they believe they might be led endlessly in a circle and never find their way out again. I don't believe it. Only children believe it.

"Willem," I say, "I want to follow this road into the forest. You won't be scared, will you?"

I can tell that it hurts for him to speak, but I believe him when he says, "I won't be scared. I always wanted to follow a Builders' road."

As bad as he looks, his eyes still glitter with a hopeful sort of excitement. Poor kid.

I take one last look out onto the plain and along the endless strip of the road. I wonder if it leads to one of the sprawling Dead Cities that I have never seen, but which travellers always say are countless east of the ocean of grass that makes up these Great Plains. I don't know if the Dead Cities exist, but if they do, what are they but the bones left behind by a dead people? They may have built cities instead of towns, but their walls are as empty as the charred remains of ours. They had no magic.

After I found Willem in that store and dragged him away from the body of his father, we found the horse that we would later decide to call Hero standing fully saddled near the door to the stable behind the store. Maybe he belonged to the shopkeep. Or maybe he belonged to some Montanan raider who had been shot off of his back in the first wave of the attack, when the men of the town still thought they had a chance. I didn't care, and I didn't hesitate. I hoisted Willem onto the horse's back and hauled myself and my stolen supplies up behind him. I didn't realize yet just how severe his wounds really were.

To get out of town on horseback, there was no choice but to take to the streets. I kicked the horse hard and he broke into a run and out into the chaos. There was smoke everywhere and the heat of burning buildings pressed in on us from all sides. Gunfire echoed from all around. Again and again, I ducked low at the sound of shots, but it was impossible to know if any were meant for me.

I turned off of the main street as quickly as I could, but not before seeing a group of people being corralled into a barred wagon by swarthy men. Most looked to be women and children. Many of the women had been stripped bare and were clothed only in ash and blood. How many of them had I known?

We sped toward the edge of town, and my heart leapt when I saw a clear street ahead of us, and beyond that an open stretch of golden grass, miraculously free of raiders. We had a chance.

But almost at once I heard the low drumroll of hooves pounding the earth in our wake. I stole a glance backward and saw that we were pursued by a Montanan with a great blonde mustache. He had a pistol in one hand and a coil of lasso in the other.

The Montanan horsemen are revered even in Nebraska for their prowess in the saddle. It is said that they can communicate with their mounts by will alone and never have need of reigns. It is said that their horses can outpace a hawk in flight. The one that chased us was alone on his horse, while our mount carried two. Hope turned to despair in an instant.

Had I been alone, I might have given up then, but this poor boy that rode before me was already splattered with the brains of his father, and all that he had ever known was burning around him. How could I just let him be taken? I spurred the horse and fixed my eyes ahead.

The wind whipped my long hair around my face, and the horse's breath throbbed like a bellows. I rode low in the saddle, my arms shielding the boy on either side, but no shots rang out behind us. Probably our pursuer thought that a young woman and an adolescent boy were ideal for the slave market and preferred to catch us rather than kill us. Or maybe he simply wanted to rape me. I'd rather he shot me than that.

We plowed forward, past the last low hovels and smokehouses at the edge of town and out onto the plain. The golden grass lashed against my boots and at the horse's legs, but his pace never slowed. The horseman had not yet let his lasso fly, and I wondered why he delayed. Surely, he wouldn't want to have to drag us back very far.

I turned my eyes back and couldn't believe what I beheld. The rider was still there, barrelling forward at a full gallop, but the distance between him and ourselves had doubled and was growing ever larger. He continued after us for a few moments more, but soon slowed his mount and turned back toward the smoking town. This stolen horse had outrun him. I could have laughed if everything that I had ever known was not now in ruins.

Tonight, we made camp on a little spur that juts off from the main course of the Builders' road. Perhaps it was even made for this purpose, since it simply rejoins the main road again a short distance ahead, and there is no evidence of any structure ever having stood here. But then again, who knows what may have stood here before the winds of time scoured it clean?

Just as I told Willem, I think it is fairly safe to build a fire here and have done so. I am glad of it all the more because it is so dark beneath these trees. Out on the plains, the moon is always there. Even the new moon and tiny crescent moons are dappled with thousands of tiny lights. I have always wondered what they are. The stories say that they are cities filled with people, sent there by the Builders, but I don't think that can be true.

It is so quiet here in this forest. Or at least, it sounds so different from anything I have ever known. The trees sway and creak. The leaves hiss when the wind blows through them. So does the grass on the plains, but the sounds are not the same.

Willem sits, bundled in his blanket and tries to get warm by the blaze. Something about his injuries has made him grow colder and colder. And no matter how many times I dress the wound, blood continues to seep from the place where the bullet entered his flesh. Each time, the layers of red, sodden fabric peel away sickeningly from his skin, and the smell is worse. I have nothing but shredded blanket to use as bandages, and my attempts to clean the wound cause him to scream and thrash. I won't put him through that tonight.

I can see him already drifting into sleep again, but I don't want him to. I am afraid that he will close his eyes and never open them again.

"Willem," I say, "you should eat something. We still have a few strips of bison and some of the cornbread we found in Hero's saddle."

"I'm not hungry," he says, opening his eyes slowly. "You should save it."

He's not wrong that we should be careful with the food. What we have won't last us more than another day, or two at the most. I hope that I can use the rifle to hunt some game in the forest, but I don't know what sort of animals live here, and I have only ever hunted bison. But Willem has barely eaten in several days, and he won't heal if he doesn't have some food.

"Please eat something," I say.

He is silent and stares into the fire for a long moment.

"If I promise to eat something, will you tell me a story?"

"I am no good at telling stories. Anyway, I don't have any good stories."

"Tell me a story about the Builders. Then I will eat."

I breathe a deep sigh and hand him a strip of bison and my water skin. "All right, let me think for a minute..."

I draw out the pause, settling back against the saddle blanket that I am using for a bedroll and close my eyes. When I can see that the delay is making him start to squirm, I begin.

"In the time of the Builders, the American Empire ruled all the lands far and wide, from Texas in the South, where people wear their guns outside their belts for all the honest world to see, and North past these Black Hills to where it is always winter, and East and West so far that there are real oceans with more water than all the buffalo in the world could ever drink. And one man ruled it all. That was the President of America.

"All of the Builders, as you well know, had enormous powers. They could talk to each other from thousands of miles away, they could fly at will, they could create feasts just by thinking about them, all kinds of things. And the President had more power than all the rest.

"But the President was fearful because he knew that others would be jealous of his position, and so he decided that he needed a fortress greater than anything that even the Builders had created before. He searched far and wide for someone who could build it for him.

"Eventually, he heard tell of a fellow named Jack Squarefoot, whom I think you may have heard of before."

Willem smiles at the mention of Jack Squarefoot. Everybody loves stories about him.

"Now, Jack Squarefoot was monstrously ugly, but he had powers that no one else had even imagined. The other Builders had often been cruel to Jack on account of his looks, so he was not himself

eager to be kind. He told the President that he would build his fortress, but only in exchange for half of the gold in America.

"The President was filled with anger. He desperately wanted the magical fortress, but he hated the idea of giving Jack half the gold in America. After thinking long and hard, he told Jack that he would agree to his terms, but only if Jack could complete the project in a week.

"Even with all of his power, Jack Squarefoot knew that he would not be able to finish the fortress in a week, but, clever as he was, he agreed and offered the President a bottle of fine whiskey to seal the deal. What the President didn't know was that the whiskey was enchanted so that every night the President drank of it he would sleep for thirty days.

"The President, who was a great lover of whiskey, of course drank a great deal of it that very first night and duly awoke a month later. He called Jack in to ask of his progress and Jack told him that he was a little behind schedule, but that there was nothing to worry about. Very pleased with himself, the President laughed and had another generous glass of the whiskey.

"Every month, the President would awake, thinking he had slept for only a single night, and call Jack in for a report. And each time, Jack would make increasingly frantic excuses for his work's slow progress. The President never thought to go and inspect the work site for himself.

"After the seventh month, which he thought was only the seventh day, the President awoke and demanded to at last see the progress Jack had made on the fortress. His retainers brought him to the site, and he was astonished to discover, fully finished, the most magnificent fortress he had ever seen. Jack Squarefoot, on the other hand, was nowhere to be seen.

"Eventually, the President discovered Jack sleeping lazily under a tree. When he woke up, he told the President that he had made excellent progress on the final day and had actually been finished for several hours.

"The President was outraged and suspected that he had been tricked, but couldn't say how. But because he had made a contract before all of the Builders, and the Builders were great lovers of contracts, he was forced to pay Jack Squarefoot half of the gold in America."

Willem smiles and claps for a second before the pain forces him to stop with a wince.

"You told it really well," he says. "Better than most times I've heard it."

"Well, I just told it the way my grandfather used to tell me." The thought of my grandfather gives my heart a twinge. He has been gone for years, but he is tied in my heart to so many other people.

Willem seems to be having similar thoughts, because he is quiet for a long while. Eventually, he says, "Mel, what happened to the Builders?"

"They all died out. You know that."

"Yeah, but what about their magic? Why didn't that save them?"

"Those are just stories. The Builders couldn't really do any of those things. They were just people. And they died, just like everyone does."

I don't mean to sound so bitter, but the hurt of everyone we have lost is still so fresh, and it's no use pretending the world is some magical place.

"Maybe you have never seen it and maybe I have never seen it, but that doesn't mean that there was never any magic! Or that there never will be again!" With that he rolls over and pulls his blanket up over his face.

Let him believe that, I think, blinking back tears. He has dealt with enough pain. Poor kid.

We've been in the Black Hills for five days now, and we still haven't found any trappers or people of any kind. But I did manage to shoot a thin, graceful animal that I think may have been a deer, so at least our food supply is holding out. I did my best to smoke as much of the meat as Hero can carry.

Willem, on the other hand, has been getting worse by the day. He is so pale now that he is almost perfectly white. I think he has entered some kind of fever. Even with all of this new food available, I can barely convince him to eat a thing. He drinks the water that I pour into his lips, and he rides sagging on Hero's back. The horse seems to be doing well.

Since we haven't seen any sign of pursuit or slaver encampments and since we have had no luck in locating friendly trappers, I am starting to wonder if we should just start looking for a place to dig in for the Winter. We have seen a few small ruins, most of them just a couple of slouching walls with no roof. But with some work, maybe one could be formed into something resembling a house. There is plenty of wood in the forest to keep a warm fire going all winter, and if I shot one deer, maybe I can shoot more. I wonder if Hero can survive Winter in a place like this.

We are approaching the crest of the hill we have been steadily climbing for some time now, and I am thinking that the top will be a good spot to survey for likely places to make a winter home. There seems to be something of a clearing ahead.

I look up at Willem on Hero's back and see that he is sleeping in the saddle again. He has been doing this more and more lately, and my stomach churns at the thought of losing him. I wish I knew how to help him.

We will stop for a rest at the crest of the hill. He can sleep a bit there, and maybe I can get him to eat a little.

When we finally reach the clearing, I know at once that this is a ruin left by the Builders. There are strange pillars jutting out of the ground at regular intervals, and the ground is strewn with perfectly square paving stones that have been wrenched out of the earth here and there by the roots of trees. The path that the stones imply seems to lead to an area right at the hill's edge. I try to wake Willem, who will be excited at such an interesting find, but he only stirs slightly at my touch.

At the end of the path, I look down and see a sight unlike anything I have ever beheld. Cut into the hillside, in the perfectly smooth stone that only the Builders could produce, is a series of terraced ledges that form an enormous half circle. They can only be seats, like a sort of stone theater facing the mountain ahead. I look up to see the mountainside and my breath freezes entirely. I have never seen anything *remotely* like it.

I shout at Willem until his heavy eyelids part, and half-help, half-drag him from Hero's saddle and down onto the topmost seat of the ruinous amphitheater. When he sees the rows of seats, he opens his eyes a bit more and murmurs, "The Builders..."

"Not that," I say. "Look," and point toward the mountain before us.

His eyes follow the the line of my finger and focus at last. Across the face of the mountain itself, carved from the stone, are four enormous faces, four men hewn in granite of unfathomable scale. Their features are strange. Their identities are unknowable. Half of one face has crumbled. But there they are, looking out over the world with eyes that have stared across countless centuries.

I look at Willem beside me and ask what he thinks. He leans heavily against my side and breathes several slow deep breaths. My eyes fill with tears at the sound.

Finally, he says, "Mel." His voice is little more than a whisper. He breathes in once more, very, very slowly. "There is magic…"

THREE TIMES FAST

BETHANY SNYDER

She hasn't thought of the nightmare in years. The last time it had woken her, breathless, her skin slick with sweat, she had been just nine years old. Then her father died, and the nightmare changed.

Now her breath quickens, her forearms marble into gooseflesh. She closes her eyes and takes a step back, directly onto Max's foot.

"Ow! Watch it," he says. He shakes his head and goes back to writing on the coffee-stained pad of paper he keeps tucked in his back pocket.

Caroline looks again, a child's peek, though she resists the urge cover her eyes with her splayed fingers. It is not just a door, it's the exact door from the nightmare that plagued her as a child, that left her screaming in the milky light of near dawn, terrifying her sister and causing Daphne — as if she needed cause — to wet the bed again. When the nightmares stopped, Caroline forgot the door completely, but now it comes into sharp and immediate focus: the burnt umber rust flakes on the hinges, the weather-beaten wood, splintered and pale gray, the color of driftwood. The knob is the worst of it, copper aged green, embellished with one of those eyeless angel faces that decorate tombstones in neglected cemeteries full of the long dead.

"Breathing is a requirement," Max says.

"What?"

"For life. Breathing. You should try it."

"I'm breathing."

"Jesus, Carrie. The look on your face right now, I mean, it's exactly what people mean when they say 'you look like you've seen a ghost.'" Max snaps a picture, and, blissfully, the light momentarily blinds her.

Caroline turns her back on the door, although that is almost worse than facing it. "Let's get out of here. I'm hungry." She isn't, but Max will do whatever she asks if food is involved.

Caroline knows that the breathing she hears behind her, ragged and shallow, is just Max (a pack-a-day smoker), but she bites down on her lower lip to squelch a scream. Copper floods her mouth. It's only five steps across the narrow room from the nightmare door to the green metal door that leads to the tunnels proper, but her feet sink in the wet cement of her terrified childhood, and each step takes approximately a year, one for each year the nightmare came.

When they are safely back in the mailroom — long vacant, a pile of 1996 Yellow Pages rotting in the corner beneath the empty mailboxes — Caroline's heart begins to slow. While Max packs the gear, Caroline risks a look back. Three steps lead down to the tunnels, which split off, left and right, to the main academic buildings on campus. In between is the green door, and behind that green door is the nightmare.

There is nothing to see but a hand-lettered sign, the tape in the corners brittle and yellowed, that reads, "Keep Out. This Means You."

When Caroline told her sister that she'd accepted a job as a location researcher for "that show with the hunky ghost-hunting brothers," Daphne hadn't laughed. Instead, she'd pleaded with Caroline not to take the job.

"You were afraid of everything. You were afraid of the *moon*," Daphne said. "And now you're going to research ghosts?"

"I was a kid!"

"Okay, so now you're fine, right? You don't have any more nightmares, no more waking up screaming? How long since Dad's made an appearance at the foot of your bed?"

Those were the nightmares that came after. When Jack Winter was still alive, Caroline was haunted by the door — a door she was sure she had seen in real life, maybe in the cellar at her grandpa's house, maybe in the dark at the end of the hallway in the library, maybe (this was the worst) at school, in the basement where they had to go for music class and the lights always flickered. Everyone told her it wasn't real, there was no door like that anywhere, but she knew. When Jack finally succumbed to the cancer that had turned him into a walking wraith during Caroline's fourth grade year, *he* became the nightmare. Daphne didn't remember the door, and Caroline did not remind her.

"That's all over, Daph. For years."

In the end, Caroline promised her sister that she would check in daily, and make an appointment with her therapist, and leave the job if it became too much. The more she researched ghosts, the less often the spectre of Jack Winter visited her dreams. The daily calls became weekly, and the therapist appointment was cancelled. Caroline made fast friends with Max, the location scout, as well as the girls who did hair and makeup. She moved into a bigger apartment and adopted a cat and started seeing a man she met at one of Max's barbecues: Dan, a financial advisor.

And then the script about the college came across her desk. They wanted something that looked classic New England, haunted, and she knew the perfect location. Bradford had been shuttered for a decade; ivy grew over the doors, books lined the shelves in the library, white linen tablecloths rotted on the round tables in the dining hall. It was as if they had turned out the lights, locked the doors, and never looked back.

And there were tunnels, as requested.

Max plucks the last handful of fries from the cardboard sleeve and dunks them in his milkshake. Chocolate dribbles into his beard.

"You are raising the bar, girl," Max says. "I mean, that place is perfect."

"Good," Caroline says. Her burger is still in its paper wrapper.

"Are you okay?" He puts his hand on top of hers. "What's wrong?"

She runs her tongue along the ridge on her lip where her teeth broke the skin. "That door," she says. "The one with the weird knob."

Max nods, flipping pages in his notebook. A smear of grease smudges the words. He's drawn a sketch of the door, hasty but accurate, and Caroline shivers. "Pretty creepy, right?"

She wants to tell Max about the nightmare, and how it is, somehow, the exact same door. She wants to tell him how, in the childhood dream, she stands in front of it, not moving, barely even breathing, and she cannot leave — she is *not allowed* to leave — until she knocks on that door, three times fast. She is frozen — five, six, eight years old — frozen to the dirt floor, paralyzed. She cannot move and she cannot leave, and she and the door face each other and wait, it creaking — almost *breathing* — and settling into the earth; she trembling, shivering in her thin nightgown, and desperately trying to not wet her pants. She knows that she must knock on the door three times fast, but she also knows, in the deepest part of her dreaming brain, that when she does, something will answer. Something big and terrible. Something with teeth. She wants to tell Max that, finally, because she has to pee *so very much*, she reaches out with one clenched fist and, her mouth frozen in a rictus of fear, feels her knuckles touch the splintered wood. And then she wakes up, shrieking.

But she can't say any of this to Max. In the overheated dining room, under the fluorescent lights, her throat closes and the most she can manage is, "I don't like it."

"Tomorrow when we meet the guy, we'll see if he can let us in."

"In?"

Max crumples the cardboard and waxy paper on his tray and lets out a quiet belch. "In the door. Don't you want to see what's inside?"

Caroline picks up coffee on her way to the campus in the morning. Her pockets are stuffed with cream and sugar, because she doesn't know how Mr. Favell likes it. She and Max both take it black.

Mr. Favell, the town historian, does not drink coffee. He is small, with a pointy nose and a scarf wrapped tight around his throat, although it is a warm day for late October. He ushers them down past the mailroom and into the tunnels, lecturing on the history of the school, admonishing them to watch where they step and to not touch the walls, which are covered with dated graffiti.

"How are we gonna shoot down here if we can't touch anything?" Max says.

Favell shines his flashlight down the left-hand tunnel, then the right. He will take them down each branch in turn, lead them in to the long-shuttered buildings where the tunnels dead end. But first, the beam of light lands on the green door.

"This room," he says, "was used to store things."

"Things," Caroline repeats. She clenches her fists in rhythm to her heartbeat, which is steady and slow. The night before, she had finally spoken aloud about the nightmare door, confessing the story to Dan after downing a bottle of wine. He put his arms around her while she cried, and then they laughed, finally, at how sure she'd been that she was going to pee her pants, and how each dawn, it was Daphne who ended up wetting the bed. Caroline thinks now, as she watches the historian pull a jangle of keys from his coat pocket, that she would like to introduce Dan to her sister.

"Things. Yes. An assortment of things," Favell says. He pushes open the green door and there is it, five steps away, the literal stuff of nightmares. Caroline focuses on the historian's face, his bristle-brush mustache that twitches as he talks. "Potatoes. Beets. Parsnips, perhaps."

Max laughs. "So you're saying this was a root cellar."

"Perhaps." Favell shifts his weight, purses his lips. "Some information is incomplete."

"What's behind that door?" Caroline asks, surprised at how easy her voice sounds.

"I have it here," Favell says. He rummages in his briefcase for a moment, and then presents a rolled blueprint. He asks Max to hold it up against the concrete block wall, and then runs his finger across it until he finds the mailroom, and then the tunnels.

Caroline steps closer and reads the handwritten text aloud: "Swimming pool?" The question mark is part of the notation.

"Ah, yes," the historian says. The mustache twitches. "In the 1950s, the administration first began considering turning the school into a four-year college for both men and women. As you undoubtedly know," he said, nodding first at Caroline and then at Max, "Bradford did not become a co-educational facility until 1971. However, as I have already mentioned, there was talk of transformation two decades earlier. At that time, plans were developed to install an underground swimming pool. Just here, behind that door."

"An underground swimming pool," Max repeats. He hands the blueprint back to Favell and digs out his notebook. "Could be a good storyline, right?" he says quietly to Caroline, who nods. Max writes screenplays in his spare time, along with half the cast and crew.

"How far did they get in building it?" Caroline asks.

The historian picks through the keys until he finds the one he's looking for. It slides easily into the hole beneath the dead angel doorknob, and Caroline hears Max inhale sharply beside her. She bites the sore spot on her lip and tries to think of the heat of the wine in her belly, the sound of Dan's laughter, the coolness of his skin as they lay in bed in the morning, shoulder to shoulder. The sunlight through the window, the smell of coffee brewing downstairs, the promise of —

There is a high-pitched scream, and then Max shouts, "Jesus Christ!"

"My good man, are you all right?" Favell says, and Caroline laughs. Max is bent over with his hands on his knees, breathing heavily.

"What the hell!" Max says. "Why did you scream?"

"I didn't scream," Caroline replies.

"Not you. Him."

In the dim light, Caroline sees the historian blush. "I was startled," he says. Twitch, twitch.

"It's a concrete wall," Max says.

"I see that now," Favell says. "Please excuse me. I just... I thought I saw something. Right as the door opened."

But there is nothing to see, nothing but a concrete wall. Solid, impenetrable. Caroline takes the camera from Max and snaps a picture, then two. She makes sure that the historian is in one of the shots. Dan will love this story, and photographic evidence will make the telling of it even better.

Favell prattles on about parsnips and the benefits of co-educational higher learning as he re-locks the door to nothing. The two men cross the narrow room to the green door, the historian fussing with his flickering flashlight, Max shoving his notebook into his pocket and shaking his head.

Caroline faces the door, her shoulders square. She waits a moment, waits for the panic, waits for the terror to loosen her bladder, but it does not come. There is nothing behind the door. Concrete, thick and solid as a tombstone. She closes her eyes and sees not the door but her father, Jack Winter, flesh over bones, the face of the wraith at the end of the bed. That dream will still come.

The men are in the mailroom now, their voices muffled. Caroline opens her eyes, steps to the door, and raises her clenched fist. As her knuckles touch the splintered wood, something knocks from the other side, three times fast.

RECOMMENDED MEMORIES FOR YOU

S. MYRSTON

LED ZEPPELIN CHICAGO 1975

A. Manson (Editor) Anonymous (Source)

♦♦♦♦♦ 97 Customer reviews

This highly acclaimed recollection, featuring both semantic and episodic tracks, relives a young man's experience, standing close to the stage of a Led Zeppelin concert at the height of their popularity. Interest in a pretty girl begins midway through the concert and escalates quickly. This interaction enhances the show with an element of sexual tension and proceeds to personalize the event.

Watch John Bonham, the finest drummer to ever beat a pigskin, work the classics with ecstatic fervor. Allow Jimmy to lead you up the stairway while the young redhead tries to suffocate you with her tongue; her 'old man' stands but a few feet away, seemingly oblivious to it all. When the concert starts drawing to a close, you realize you have a choice to make: Wait for the encore Zeppelin has in store, or seek out one of your own making; with a girl who clearly seems up for it; with a Ford Mustang that's still in pristine condition; with a back pocket full of illegal substances; without prophylactics in your wallet nor any need for them.

Please be aware, this piece can be dangerous to your mental wellbeing. You might just remember what a real redhead can do with limited space and a set of lips the next time your wife turns out the lights on date night; You might realize the radio has never held any purpose in your lifetime other than to fill the spaces between adverts; your dealer doesn't have the good stuff and never has; the musicians you idolized are talentless; your modern, air-conditioned, air-bagged car is essentially feminine; your father had a better lifestyle than you ever had or will. You might come to know what the cost of progress has been, and who is paying it.

- Run time: 4 hours.
- Format: PCCEB (Full Semantic and Episodic tracks)
- Quality: 6-8 GBS.
- Price: $120
- Olfactory triggers: Marijuana, human perspiration
- Rating: 18+, contains explicit content of a sexual nature

All purchases are subject to terms and conditions. Reminsc.co.za cannot guarantee the quality of interface with cerebral play and similar devices. Not for sale to residents of USA, South Korea or the EU.

Most Recent Customer Comments:

Fapman: ♦♦♦♦♦ *First.*

infin8: ♦♦♦♦ *Awesome. My favorite was 'Whole Lot of Love' & Bonham losing the plot in the drum solo. That and shtooping the redhead, obviously. She was wild.*

RvdB: ♦♦♦♦♦ *Great stint. Except mine kept fading out every few minutes. I have an older ceb interface but never had problems before. Is there a way to reduce the GBS to play on older systems?*

Fapman: ♦♦♦♦ *I think I just shagged my Gran. Anyone know a good psychiatrist?*

XXL: ♦♦♦♦ *BEST. BAND. EVER. JUST ONE COMMENT: GET THAT GIRL A RAZOR. HER PUBES STARTED AT HER NAVAL AND ENDED AT HER KNEES. LOL*

L4665: ♦♦♦♦ *OMG. Best nyt of my Lyf. weL not myn bt U knO wot i mean I alwys hErd ppl goin on bout Zeppelin & thawt dey wer pretentious twats bt nw I undRstNd wot d fuss wz bout. Y can't any1 mAk music lIk DIS anymore? agrE w xxl tho — dey nEd 2 git dat grl razor.*

F_T: ♦♦♦♦ *@L4665; @ XXL. You're fucking morons. It's not directed or scripted. It's a historic piece. A real fucking memory. That's what girls were like in the day.*

JackyD: ♦♦♦♦ *@F_T, I think they know that. They just think the experience would have been better with the girl more like the child-like, fake-breasted, shaved women that they are used to masturbating to on modern porn websites.*

Lisa T. ♦♦♦♦ *Always been a massive Led-head, now even more so than ever. I never realized how hot Page was. I'd let him use a shark on me any day.*

Best Sellers | Historic | Deals | **Educational** | Music | Spiritual | Travel | Romance | Submissions

FRENCH IN A WEEK
A. Steyn (Editor) E. Sinclar (Source)
♦♦♦♦ 112 Customer reviews

'French in a Week' does just what is promises. Cebing this series for three hours a day, for seven consecutive days, will leave you fully conversant in this intricate and colorful language. Giving you all the benefits of speaking French (sophistication and confidence) without any of the drawbacks of actually having to be French (poor personal hygiene and general misanthropy.)

These recorded memories feature a young French woman speaking while walking the streets of Paris. She starts by simply pronouncing names of objects she comes across, allowing your mind to quickly establish a vocabulary. Gradually she expands words into phrases and then into sentences. The later sessions are mostly conversations with random Parisians. Learning to speak French in this manner, employing muscle and phonetic memory, your pronunciation will be more authentic than most expats ever achieve in their lifetimes.

With your newly acquired skills go ahead and accurately describe the insects inhabiting your bed to the hotel concierge. Haggle with prostitutes effectively or explain in detail, to the waiter, what he can go and do to his own mother. Order previously unspeakable acts to be carried out on geese with impeccable pronunciation. This series will make you a French speaker for the rest of your life, provide insight into Paris itself and save you from having to read all those subtitled movies your wife makes you watch.

- Run time: 7 x 3 hours.
- Format: PCCEB (Episodic track only)
- Quality: 14 GBS.
- Price: $699
- Olfactory triggers: Coffee, Garlic, Urine, Human perspiration.
- Rating: 18+, contains explicit language.

All purchases are subject to terms and conditions. Reminsc.co.za cannot guarantee the quality of interface with cerebral play and similar devices. Not for sale to residents of USA, South Korea or the EU.

Most Recent Customer Comments:

Aceshigh: ♦ *Seventh language and counting. This has to be the most exciting "..in a Week" piece I have completed. I recommend this if for no other reason than the cursing. They have words for things you wouldn't even think of in English.*

ALF2You: ♦♦♦♦♦ *French is physically difficult to pronounce for an English speaker. My tongue and mouth struggles to mouth several words in French. Tongue fatigue: It's a thing.*

NorthofI: ♦♦♦♦♦ *Why is this sooo expensive? I can either go to France or learn to speak French but I can't afford to do both.*

ALF2You: ♦♦♦♦♦ *@Northof, 700 bucks is not expensive. You would pay way more for the audio books or for French lessons and afterwards you would still barely know how to speak the language. For all of you insulting France or the French: Nique ta mere.*

NathanP ♦♦♦♦♦ *I studied French at school for five years and could barely say hello (it was a decade ago) Now, after two weeks with the Cebtech I'm better than my any of my old teachers. @UK2U, I agree it is a tongue twister at first. Took me a full month of practicing before my tongue caught up with my mind.*

Julie8teen: ♦ *France is a fantastic country, it's only Paris that sucks. Get out of the big cities and into the countryside and the people are super friendly and kind. The landscapes are gorgeous and the food is great, not like the pretentious, overpriced crap they assemble in Paris. Stacking food into neat circular piles doesn't make it taste better.*

Go2grnd: ♦♦♦♦♦ *I went to Paris after watching this. I was able to remember my way around the city, speak to people I met and order food at restaurants. I don't think I would have had half as much fun if I hadn't watched this before.*

Best Sellers | Historic | Deals | Educational | Music | **Spiritual** | Travel | Romance | Submissions

EVERYTHING ZEN

M. Tonges (Editor) Anonymous (Source)
♦♦♦♦♦ 412 Customer reviews

A nameless Buddhist monk sits down in a Tibetan monastery, closes his eyes and enters into a meditative state. He maintains resonating alpha and theta patterns for three hours during which he contemplates two koans. This rare piece offers almost no visual nor auditory stimuli however the emotional states employed by the subject is transferred to the recipients mind with varying degrees of success. To those open to the experience, a deep sense of enlightenment can be achieved.

Take advantage of years of focused and disciplined mental training by an experienced and dedicated master of contemplative meditation. Open yourself to a spiritual awareness, loss of self and an overwhelming sense of unity with the universe. This piece is largely responsible for a recent upsurge in eastern philosophy in western popular culture. This is the one everyone has been talking about. Oprah called it "life altering." Snoop claims it was the catalyst in shifting to his new persona: "Brother Dog." Katy Perry claimed it allowed her to achieve a state "not unlike happiness" for the first time in her adult life. Harvested by M Tonges, editor of the highly acclaimed "Killers Garden" and "Masai Hunt."

This piece has been proven to reduce stress, hypertension, and hemorrhoids in a recent double blind study conducted by a prominent Swiss university. Side effects may include lethargy, veganism, mild telepathy, and in rare cases adult-onset-ponytails in males.

- Run time: 3.5 hours.
- Format: PCCEB (Full Semantic and Episodic tracks)
- Quality: 14-18 GBS.
- Price: $69
- Olfactory triggers: Wild grass, herbal tea
- Rating: Parental Guidance Suggested

All purchases are subject to terms and conditions. Reminsc.co.za cannot guarantee the quality of interface with cerebral play and similar devices. Not for sale to residents of USA, South Korea or the EU.

Most Recent Customer Comments:

Fapman: ♦ *Yawn. I want my money back and the two hours of my life lost listening to static.*

Jack: ♦♦♦♦♦ *Does no one learn from history? This sort of eastern esoteric shit led to some of the worst albums of all time. Turning perfectly good bands into self-centered sitar-playing douchebags. If it can happen to the Beatles and Alanis Morisette it can happen to anyone. Imagine how bad the next Nickleback album is going to be if they buy into this?*

Go2grnd: ♦♦♦♦♦ *I thought it was incredible except for that plonker who keeps hitting you with a plank just when you're about to have a breakthrough. What the fuck was that about?*

Fapman: ♦ *@Jack, I wouldn't worry about it, Nickleback wouldn't break the law. They drive the speed limit, enjoy monogamous relationships and get their highs on life and bottled water.*

IATW: ♦♦♦♦♦ *How can Oprah and Snoop claim to have recollected this? Isn't it illegal? Aren't they admitting guilt?*

Fapman: ♦ *Mhhmmm Alriiiighty then.*

Go2grnd: ♦♦♦♦♦ *@IATW, Only in the US. If they watched this in another country, there's nothing they legally have to worry about.*

Backtrack: ♦♦♦♦ *I heard that this is actually Richard Gere meditating. It could be – you never see his face.*

Milue83 : ♦♦♦♦♦ *You are all such cynics. This was a life changing piece for me. I would never have even called myself 'spiritual' but after watching this I feel changed, connected to something and small. I am no longer a unique and special being. I don't believe the above commentators actually watched this memory. If they did, they are jaded beyond repair.*

VIEW FROM THE TOP 1973

J. Digruber (Editor) Z. Greengold (Source)

♦♦♦♦ 412 Customer reviews

It's 1973 and a young Israeli soldier, Zvika Greengold, is at home on leave to celebrate Yom Kippur. When word of a surprise, coordinated attack from Egypt and Syria throws the country into chaos, Zvika proceeds to hitchhike to a deserted base in the Golan Heights to take command of an outdated centurion tank with but a couple of other soldiers.

Remember, as Zvika, as he scouts a full Syrian tank brigade advancing unopposed towards Nafekh. Zvika, unwilling to call command for help, out of fear or announcing the gaping hole in Israel's defense, decides to engage this overwhelming force on his own, in an attempt to slow their advance.

The very fate of your country hangs in the balance. It's going to be a tank battle the likes of which the world has never seen. It's you against an army. It's going to require unorthodox tactics, tireless aggression and bravery bordering on suicidal tenacity. It's going to be a very long day.

- Run time: 8 hours.
- Format: PCCEB (Full Semantic and Episodic tracks)
- Quality: 6-8 GBS.
- Price: $89
- Olfactory triggers: Cordite. Human Perspiration
- Rating: 18+, contains explicit content of a sexual and violent nature

All purchases are subject to terms and conditions. Reminsc.co.za cannot guarantee the quality of interface with cerebral play and

S. Myrston · 76

similar devices. Not for sale to residents of USA, South Korea or the EU.

Most Recent Customer Comments:

Backtrack: ◆◆◆◆◆ *I've heard this story a hundred times from my dad but I had no idea how much this man did for his country. I realize not everyone will take it the same way because, to me it was extremely personal. I found it to be profound, almost a spiritual journey.*

Chicago4: ◆◆◆◆ *Why is this technology still illegal in the states? It's been around in Asia for five years but you can still get put away for decades here. Switzerland has this in schools and public libraries. Here — they don't even talk about it in mainstream media. WHY???*

Kasey: ◆◆◆◆◆ *Epic. Like '300' but with tanks.*

Isman ◆ *Zionist propaganda — I don't believe a minute of this. It's clearly been cut up to show only the pieces which suit the Zionist agenda. I always thought that memories couldn't be faked but now I'm not so sure.*

BBack64 ◆◆◆◆ *Is this story really true? If so, why haven't they made a movie about this?*

F_T: ◆◆◆◆ *It's Jewish Die Hard. With mechanized armor. Everything it better with mechanized armor. Yom Kippur-ki-yay motherfucker.*

JPsandrs ◆◆◆◆ *Why have I never heard of this guy before?*

lAce82 ◆◆ *Quality was terrible and even when it wasn't — I can't speak Hebrew!!!*

Isman ◆ *Why not record the slaughter and invasion of Palestine or the forced removal of thousands? What about the*

Jewish artillery, cluster bombs and orchestrated genocide of the only nuclear power in the Middle East? Why Israel is allowed nuclear weapons while North Korea or Iran is not is nothing but hypocrisy.

BBack64 ◆◆◆◆ *Why does Israel have nuclear weapons? Because they invented them. If you don't believe me, read the list of names from the Manhattan Project.*

JPsandrs: ◆◆ *@ Chicago4: One word: "Snowden" He was one of the first to have his memories extracted. They're worried everyone will learn the truth.*

Best Sellers | Historic | Deals | **Educational** | Music | Spiritual | Travel | Romance | Submissions

ICH BIN EIN GERMAN

M. Arsenault (Editor) M. Tyralla (Source)
◆◆◆◆ 412 Customer reviews

As great as they are, *Inglourious Basterds* and Internet pornography are hardly a comprehensive representation of German culture. Sure, they may have started a tiff of two in their time, but they also gave the world Heidi Klum and automobiles. They're clearly trying hard to be nicer, as a nation, and haven't initiated any global conflicts in over seventy years.

Germany has been one of the most important, influential cultures of the western psyche and innovators of science, art, literature and manufacturing since the Middle Ages. Now you can learn to speak Deutsch as a German in three weeks. The training is given by a lovely, young native Frankfurter, M Tyralla, who is clearly proud of her culture and language.

If you've never had a beer served to you in a Munich beerhall by a buxom, dirndl-clad blonde then you have never experienced beer the way God intended. Develop an appreciation for the Hoff on a more profound level. Understand the origins or your favorite sausages. Settle the famous "citizen of Berlin/Jelly Doughnut" incident in your own mind, once and for all. Intimidate your mechanic the next time he tries to pull one over on you.

Once completed, you will be able to identify and insult Fish-heads, Ossies and Valley shitters with such genuine pronunciation we guarantee you will be punched hard, in the mouth at least once per incident. And of course, if you ever met Heidi or Claudia, how better would your chances be if you could hit on her in her home language?

In rare cases, learning German has resulted in a strange psychological need to mimic the walking patterns of the person in front of you. Others have noticed increased anxiety levels while playing strategy board games such as Risk, chess and Game of Thrones.

- Run time: 25 hours.
- Format: PCCEB (Full Semantic and Episodic tracks)
- Quality: 7-10 GBS.
- Price: $129
- Olfactory triggers: Beer, Pickled Herring
- Rating: All Ages

All purchases are subject to terms and conditions. Reminsc.co.za cannot guarantee the quality of interface with cerebral play and similar devices. Not for sale to residents of USA, South Korea or the EU.

Most Recent Customer Comments:

Kasey: ♦♦♦♦♦ *How hot was that girl? Sie war sehr sexy.*

H8M8: ♦♦♦♦ *I went to Berlin two years ago. I would have loved to be able to speak German to those artistic waif-like students stationed at each and every bar and nightclub. That way when they told me to fuck off – I could have appreciated it on a much deeper level.*

JPsandrs: ◆◆◆◆◆ *I am a jelly doughnut.*

Bart: ◆◆◆◆◆ *Great, now all the right-winged, jack-booted, white-power fucknuts of the world will be able to read Meinkamph in the original German. A small goosestep backwards for mankind.*

Jack: ◆◆◆◆◆ *Just because you can speak German like someone from Frankfurt doesn't mean you will have any clue what someone from Bremen is saying. That's like an American understanding someone from Manchester. Not fucking likely. The accents, pronunciation and slang used is very different.*

MRebohm: ◆◆◆◆◆ *@Jack – people from Bremen do not have accents, that's how the language sounds when it's spoken correctly. Any people south of Berlin are not proper Germans anyway, they are Austrians. And Austrians are so far south they are basically Italians. Italians talk with their hands because they know how retarded the Italian language sounds and are embarrassed by it.*

Kasey: ◆◆◆◆◆ *@JPsandrs – No you aren't. You never have been and never will be, that doughnut crap was debunked long ago and only morons still cling to that version.*

Best Sellers | **Historic** | Deals | Educational | Music | Spiritual | Travel | Romance | Submissions

WESTGATE MALL, KENYA, 2013

M.D. Williamson (Editor) A.Y. Haji (Source)

◆◆◆◆ 27 Customer reviews

Abdul Yusuf Haji, a Kenyan businessman was in a meeting when he received a text from his brother trapped in a local shopping center under siege by Muslim fundamentalists. Excusing himself from the meeting, Abdul proceeds directly to the shopping center, to help his brother. There, with a small group of like-minded citizens, they advance on the mall to provide cover fire, allowing injured civilians to be rescued from the car park.

Then, an hour after the shooting began, and with the terror response team still not on site, this brave group decides to enter the mall to confront the threat and help as many people as they can. Advance with Abdul and others as they make their way through the fallen. Watch as they help lead dozens to freedom and witness the bravery as they confront the savage face of fundamentalism.

It's a confusing time as it's unclear as to who is attacking, how many, or their locations within the building. They extremists have spent the last hour killing every man, woman and child they came across who couldn't quote from the Koran. Bodies are strewn about the shops, aisles and food courts. Abdul and his fellow vigilantes only have handguns while the militants are armed with automatic rifles, grenades and suicide vests. These are battle-hardened extremists with no expectation of living beyond that day.

Watch as Abdul, a Muslim himself, advances into the mall, engaging with the terrorists and risking his life to do it. A truly inspirational and heroic event which hasn't received the attention it so richly deserves.

- Run time: 3 hours.
- Format: PCCEB (Full Semantic and Episodic tracks)
- Quality: 9 GBS.
- Price: $98
- Olfactory triggers: Cordite, human perspiration, perfume.
- Rating: 18+, explicit content of a violent nature

All purchases are subject to terms and conditions. Reminsc.co.za cannot guarantee the quality of interface with cerebral play and similar devices. Not for sale to residents of USA, South Korea or the EU.

Most Recent Customer Comments:

NeilDGT: ♦♦♦♦♦ *Brave Men. All of them.*

Jackyo: ♦♦♦♦ *Does anyone know if the cop with the AK who got shot survived?*

Rightime ♦♦♦♦♦ *Incredible – They must have saved fifty people. Where the hell was the army/swat?*

HarryM: ♦♦♦♦ *This guy was a Muslim. Taking on other Muslims – Maybe there is hope for us yet.*

XXL: ♦♦♦♦ *@HarryM – What they didn't tell you that the terrorists were questioning the people in the mall, if the people could recite from the Koran they were let go, if not they were shot. Man, woman and child. Islam is the most violent religion on the planet.*

L4665: ♦♦♦♦ *Damn – it's one thing to think you would be brave or heroic in a situation like this, but it's another thing to actually do it. Kudos to this man. What he did was incredible. The fact that he was a Muslim himself proves that most do not believe in murder and are peaceful, worthy citizens.*

F_T: ♦♦♦♦ *That's what they want you to believe – Did you know Haji was the son of the former Kenyan Defense minister. Doesn't that sound a bit dodgy?*

Jack: ♦♦♦♦ *@F_T, Bullshit, sure he may have been the son of the minister but he clearly did what he did. He is clearly a hero and your conspiracy bullshit was disproved in the memory. Watch it – then comment on it douchebag.*

A SÂU VALLEY, VIETNAM, 1966

T. Spedman (Editor) B.G. Adkins (Source)

◆◆◆◆ 227 Customer reviews

If you're a patriotic American, then you undoubtedly enjoy a good war, and as far as good wars go, Vietnam has to be one of your greatest, except for, you know, losing it. Almost three million Americans served in Vietnam, and of those, over nine hundred went on to write of their experiences. Of those nine hundred published novels, 88 were made into movies. Of those movies, only one was selected for a Cebtech memory extraction. This is the story of that memory.

Wake on the 9th of March, 1966, as Bennie Adkins, a 32 year old American member of the 5th Special Forces stationed along the Ho Chi Minh trail not far from Laos. Not a particularly safe location at that point in time. Bennie is one of only seventeen Americans "advising" the 400 strong South Vietnamese Militia when a Viet Cong force numbering in the thousands falls upon the makeshift base. Wake to the sounds of incoming indirect fire and the screams from wounded comrades.

Bennie, at this point, decides to take a more hands-on approach with regards to his advisory role. Watch as he mans a mortar with devastating effect while suffering hit after hit on his position. Listen as he rallies troops floundering against overwhelming numbers. Watch him pull the wounded to safety while taking a barrage of sniper and mortar fire and then again when he decides to make a run for additional ammunition. It quickly becomes apparent why this man was awarded the highest military honors possible.

Later that day, a significant number of South Vietnamese troops experience a miraculous epiphany regarding their political ideologies. All simultaneously realizing that they are, in fact, communists at heart and not the freedom loving, capitalistic democrats they had previously aligned themselves with.

With this treachery unfolding, with the massive shift in numbers and the renewal of mortar and small-arms fire, Bernie has no choice but to withdraw and abandon the base. Extracting the remaining survivors, they flee into the jungle where they proceed to spend the next two days avoiding VC troops, negotiating a deadly environment and avoiding man-fucking-eating tigers. Seriously. Man-fucking-eating tigers. I know.

This piece is nothing like the Vietnam you have come to know and love in the movies. This is unforgiving, desperate and overwhelming; a struggle for survival amidst the naked horrors of battle. A true reflection of the conflict and a painful reminder of why war is almost always a bad idea, but if you absolutely have to have one, then make sure you take people like Bennie with you.

- Run time: 5 hours.
- Format: PCCEB (Full Semantic and Episodic tracks)
- Quality: 14 GBS.
- Price: $88
- Olfactory triggers: Cordite, human perspiration.
- Rating: 18+, contains explicit content of a violent nature

All purchases are subject to terms and conditions. Reminsc.co.za cannot guarantee the quality of interface with cerebral play and similar devices. Not for sale to residents of USA, South Korea or the EU.

Most Recent Customer Comments:

NeilDGT: ♦ *I found this description of the memory to be truly offensive. I will not purchase from Reminisc again. They can go and screw themselves. A lot of good men died over there. Fighting communism and its cruel, oppressive regimes was a hard choice but to say it wasn't worth fighting is offensive to those who died.*

Debased4 ♦♦♦ *It's so easy to judge in hindsight. I believe the average American is against war in any form. We as a nation are not warmongers, only our politicians are. (And maybe some Republicans)*

HarryP: ♦♦♦♦ *@debased, Bullshit, Bush went to war under false pretenses and America still re-elected him. So over fifty percent of Americans are fans of war. If that doesn't convince you then nothing will.*

XXL: ♦♦♦♦ *"In the councils of government, we must guard against the acquisition of unwarranted influence, whether sought or unsought, by the military-industrial complex. The potential for the disastrous rise of misplaced power exists and will persist." D.D Eisenhower, 1961*

L4665: ♦♦♦ *"Now I am become Death, the destroyer of worlds" – Robert Oppenheimer, perhaps on America's behalf?*

Debased4: ♦♦♦♦ *@L4665: "Now I am become Death" Seriously? Grammar much?*

SPEAK US ENGLISH

Cebable International (Editor)

J.H Santiago, J. Goldrat, P. Earp (Sources)

◆◆◆◆◆ 1222 Customer reviews

English is only the third most popular language in the world today but if you can't speak the first two, Mandarin and Spanish, the locals aren't going to assume you're an idiot, like how the English speakers are going to.

Most international companies now insist their new hires speak English and it remains the most popular second language being taught to school children and adults internationally. Although America doesn't speak English properly, they have helped to popularize their version of it by frequently invading countries and teaching it within those 'liberated' territories. Just like the British used to do before them.

This piece features three native speakers explaining the basics of vocabulary, pronunciation and grammar. A New Yorker, Los Angeleno and Denverite take you through one hour sessions on a rotational basis, presumably to reduce your chances of picking up a hideous accent. The experts select landmarks within their cities to conduct their lessons, often explaining about the locations and interacting with the locals. Together, they will have you speaking English clearly within three short weeks.

America itself is beautiful country and for the most part, safe and easy to travel within. If you're planning on visiting, being able to speak to the locals will greatly enhance your experience. America is a massive, heterogeneous country. The cultures vary from state to state, some of which are populated with warm, compassionate people while others are home to armed, aggressive products of their environment.

Then again, if you aren't planning on travelling, it's important to note that it's probably the Republicans turn at the White House again starting in 2016. With another Bush as their likely candidate, your ability to speak to your captors fluently while being water-boarded is going to be more important than ever.

- Run time: 40 hours
- Format: PCCEB (Full Semantic and Episodic tracks)
- Quality: 14 GBS.
- Price: $820
- Olfactory triggers: None
- Rating: All Ages

All purchases are subject to terms and conditions. Reminsc.co.za cannot guarantee the quality of interface with cerebral play and similar devices. Not for sale to residents of USA, South Korea or the EU.

Most Recent Customer Comments:

Fapman: ◆◆◆◆◆ *At least Bush did something in his term. Obama has been the most ineffectual president the country has ever had.*

Meesters: ◆◆◆ *@ Fapman: Doing evil doesnt trump doing nothing. Besides the only reason why Obama did nothing was cause they made it theyre mission to prevent him from passing laws. Its petty politics and shows they are more interesting in their careers and influence than they are in people. The people are nothing but cattle to them.*

JUU67: ◆◆◆ *My brother's wife works from home and makes $300 per hour doing simple marketing. More people needed urgently.*

She just bought herself new Porshe. Visit www.work4hm.co.ru for more information.

JesusDelag ♦♦♦ *This was wonderful course. I am learning quickly and look forward to speaking fluently. Reminisc Rocks!*

RoB4666: ♦♦♦♦♦ *Way to suck up. I've been to America, land of crack whores and meth heads. That bullshit you're spewing about Americans being kind and smart is pure fiction.*

Acesfor8: ♦♦♦♦ *@RoB – Go fuck yourself. You know why we invade countries? Because we can.*

Best Sellers | Historic | Deals | Educational | Music | Spiritual | Travel | Romance | **Submissions**

SUBMISSIONS

S. Myrston (CEO)

Here at Reminisc, we're always looking for new and interesting memories to expand our library. Please allow me to stress the "new and interesting" part of that sentence. The miracle of birth is, surprisingly, neither. Nor is skydiving, weddings, snorkeling or making love to mildly attractive girls. Similarly, regardless of the view counts on YouTube, we don't care about anything your cat has ever done or will ever do.

But if you visited interesting places, especially a long time ago, we would love to hear from you. Perhaps you met your wife on an epic journey or spoke to the Rain Queen in Swaziland; danced with royalty on the banks of the Somme; followed the dead for a summer; listened to Coltrane; wrote a bestseller; hacked NASA; did hard time; served in an armed conflict; hunted the big five or climbed Mount Everest; if so, we would love to hear from you.

There are numerous sites peddling violent and pornographic memories today. We are not one of them. If your submission contains violence we will notify the appropriate authorities and pass along any incriminating materials. The pornographic submissions tend to be pilfered by our staff for their own sordid purposes (We know it's you, Neil.)

We offer above-market standard rates for interesting and clear recordings but for exceptional or historically significant pieces, we will enter into negotiations to ensure you receive a fair percentage of the sales.

When submitting, please send mail to: myrston_reminisc@outlook.com with a brief description of the memories and why you believe them to be special. Please do not send unsolicited data files of memories, we will not view them. Just send us the description first, if we find it intriguing, we will get back to you.

Memories are extremely personal. We get that. Sharing them could be a traumatic and intrusive experience for anyone. So if you do not have access to a good extraction system, we have global teams who can visit you in the comfort of your home to help you. Our teams have been carefully screened and trained to ensure confidentiality and professionalism.

Although exceptions are made on occasion, it's extremely unlikely any work lower than 8GBS will be considered for any category. Similarly full semantic and episodic tracks would be expected in most cases. The quality of a memory is influenced by the age and the personal significance of the event. Some mental and physical ailments can also impact the clarity, including: senility, strokes, substance abuse, hypertension or traumatic brain injuries. If in doubt, reach out to us.

We encourage and pay scouts a standard ten percent finder's fee. So if you have a relative or friend with interesting memories, speak to them and we will make it worth your while. There are people around the world who make a living doing just that. So the least you could do is speak to your grandfather and grandmother. The human race is losing precious memories every day, with every death the world forgets. Help us to prevent this from happening and we will pay you handsomely for your contributions.

ABOUT THE AUTHORS

A recent graduate of Lesley University's MFA in Creative Writing program, **S.E. Clark** lives in an old Victorian house outside of Boston with two cats and several ghosts.

S. Myrston is a South African writer previously published in *SQ Magazine*, *Star Quake 1*, *Something Wicked*, and in *African Pens: New Writing From Southern Africa 2007*, where stories were selected by Nobel Laureate J.M. Coetzee.

Bethany Snyder is a voiceover artist, a photographer, a certified personal trainer, a half-marathon walker and coach, a Maine enthusiast, and a serious pop-culture junkie. But above all, she is a writer. She writes both adult and middle-grade fiction from her home in Western New York.

Josiah Spence is a founding editor of the independent poetry journal *Rust and Moth*. His work has been published or is forthcoming in *Rare Magazine*, *Typehouse Magazine*, and *Vine Leaves*. He lives, writes, and tinkers in the great state of Texas.

R.J. Wolfe (MFAW in Creative Writing, BA in Transpersonal Studies and Writing), a playwright and fiction writer working with myths and fairytales, has published in *The Artifice*, an online magazine that covers a wide spectrum of art forms.